THE MORNING SIDE

A Two Roads Home Novel

James G. Brown

EMERGING AUTHORS

Cover Art ©Tom Clark
http://tomclarkportraits.com

Cover typeset by Sabrina Watts at Enchanted Ink Studios
www.enchanteddesigns.com

Published by Bair Ink Books
Fredericksburg, Virginia, USA
www.BairInk.com

Dedicated to my brother, Paul,
who would have if he could have.

PRAISE FOR
THE MORNING SIDE

"I LOVED THE BOOK! I CAN'T WAIT UNTIL THE NEXT INSTALLMENT!"

—Suzanne Talbot, New Hampshire

"SO MUCH TO ENJOY IN THIS POWERFUL GENERATIONAL STORY... THE RESTORATIVE POWER OF NATURE AND THE PRESSURES OF FAMILY, FRIENDS, ROMANCE AND SOCIETY ARE POIGNANTLY RELATIVE. BROWN'S MAGIC WITH WORDS BRING BOTH JERRY AND DAVID'S JOURNEYS ALIVE."

—Charles Covington, Arizona

"NARRATIVE RHYTHM IS QUICK WITH GOOD DESCRIPTIONS... DAILY LIFE DETAILS THAT ALLOW US TO QUICKLY BECOME IMMERSED IN LOCAL LIFE."

—Lucia Frick, Ontario , Canada

ACKNOWLEDGMENTS

I am indebted to many friends for the time and thoughtfulness they gave to their review and support for this book. A special thanks to Ardyth Scott and Charles Burnell.

I'm grateful to my wife, Camilla, for encouraging me and for sharing me with these characters for so many years, and I am grateful to those who offered their own perspectives on the life and times I have tried to capture, including Diane Bruce, Robert Fincham, William Jones Jr., and Jake Carle. I hasten to add that any errors or liberties with the facts in this novel are my own.

Finally, to Mary-Sherman Willis for her editorial assistance and for her dogged determination to convert me from report writer to storyteller. It is my sincere hope that readers will find that she succeeded.

"For last year's words belong to last year's language
And next year's words await another voice."

—T.S. Eliot, "Little Gidding"

PROLOGUE

APRIL 1935

Eight-year-old Gerald stepped off the porch of the Fletcher cabin with a bucket in each hand and started up the path toward the spring. He shivered as the damp morning air banished the last remnants of sleep. There was mist among the trees on the lower slopes, but the sun had begun to warm the high path where his older brother Aidan had gone earlier to check on the cattle, and he knew it would be waiting for him at the little pool to take the chill from his arms and face. Chores were so much easier now that spring was here.

Fletchers had lived in this hollow on the eastern slopes of the Blue Ridge Mountains for four generations, tending cattle from the Francis Thornton Valley every summer on a hundred acres of mountain meadows and woods. The animals fared well in the cooler climate and their owners seldom bothered to visit. Each spring they drove the cattle up the track into the hollow and, in the fall, they returned with a crew to herd them back. For the rest, like other large landowners in the region, they depended on the mountain families.

The Fletchers and their neighbors were the keepers of these mountains. Nothing was written (many couldn't write) but they kept the dirt tracks passable and the meadows clear of encroaching brush. They maintained the stone and chestnut rail fences that crisscrossed the rugged terrain. They fought the brush fires started by lightning and rebuilt the watering holes after a flash flood. When a rogue bear took a calf, they made sure it didn't happen again.

Gerald had visited the lowland. He was in awe of its big farms and fancy houses, and the general store down in Sperryville certainly had a lot more candy to choose from than Mrs. Ball's front-room shop over in Hazel Hollow. But the mountains were home. His sense of belonging was defined as much by the rhythm of their days and seasons as it was by his mother's touch or his father's voice.

On the way to the spring, he paused briefly to check on the fiddleheads that had sprouted along a bank below the path. He made a note to tell his mother that they were just about ready to pick and smiled to himself at the thought of how good they would taste the way she fixed them, with fatback and a touch of vinegar.

As he crouched on the path, Gerald became aware of a sound that didn't fit in. *A truck—no, two vehicles; maybe a truck and a car—on the road heading up the hollow toward the house. Visitors?* he thought, *But who could it be this early?* Everyone had morning chores just like the Fletchers, and business and friendship alike generally waited until the chores were done.

Curiosity began to get the better of him, but he was not about to return to the house without the morning water. The very idea conjured images of discipline... a slap to the back of his head that would go on from there depending on how his father's day was going. So, feet flying and buckets jostling, he raced the last fifty yards to the spring.

It seemed like forever before the buckets were filled and he could start back down the path. If only he could just dip them in the water and go, but to avoid getting leaves and such in the buckets, he had been taught to fill them slowly using a hollow gourd that hung from a limb by the water.

When he finally did approach the edge of the clearing, loud voices cut through the trees.

Then an angry scream from his mother.

He stopped and slipped out of sight behind a small cedar tree, trying to make sense of the confusion below.

Two men in sheriff's uniforms held his father by the arms and were forcing him away from the house. A man, in what looked like an old army uniform, was restraining his mother as best he could while trying to protect himself as she slapped and kicked at him furiously. Two others in the same uniform stood nearby, looking around anxiously. Chloe, his five-year-old sister, clutched a sack of chicken feed, terrified and crying.

His mother, Ruby, swore at the intruders and lashed out again at the one trying to hold her. She caught him squarely enough in the groin that he released her and dropped to his knees. Flashing a threat at the other two men that froze them where they stood, she reached to comfort her daughter.

The deputies had taken Gerald's father to the other side of the yard and when Ruby saw that they were handcuffing him to an oak tree next to the woodpile she let out a stream of profanities. Reaching for a garden fork that lay by the path, she made for the deputies.

Up on the hillside, Gerald started to move. He had to do something; he had no idea what, but this chaos had to stop. He was about to launch his small frame down the hill when, without looking up, his mother hurled an order at the surrounding forest.

"Boys! Stay where you are."

She knew Gerald and Aidan would be back momentarily. They would be useless against five men and she might need someone to go get help when this thing was over. So, Gerald watched in frightened silence as his father snarled threats at the men who were heading back toward the house, toward his mother, still advancing with her fork at the ready.

A flash of motion registered on the periphery of Gerald's vision. His eyes caught up with it just as Dodger left the ground, flying at the nearest deputy. The dog's arrival was a sure sign that Aidan was back, watching from somewhere nearby.

The searing growl must have added to the man's terror as he wheeled around, coming face to face with the threat flying toward him. Only the instinctive raising of his arm protected the man's throat from the hound's teeth, which set like a vice on his forearm, tearing to the bone as the animal's weight bore the man to the ground.

Dodger had done his duty, but he had also changed the rules. The other deputy drew his pistol and hurried toward the flailing arms and legs. Launching a kick from behind, he caught Dodger's flank. The dog spun away from the downed man to face the new threat and when the gun went off the bullet tore into Dodger's chest, dropping him where he stood.

Only Gerald's ingrained obedience kept him in his hiding place.

He huddled down with his arms wrapped around his knees, the sour taste of fear welling up in his throat. As he rocked back and forth in bewildered silence, tears began to track down his face.

Down in the yard, the shock of the gunfire transfixed everyone for a moment. His mother dropped the garden fork and knelt by the dog as he drew his last faint breaths. Gerald's father stood limply, shaking his head.

"Why are you doin' this?" he asked, more a plea than a question. "This here's our home! You know it's our home."

"You know the law, Jake," the senior deputy replied. "You were given time to sign the papers and leave on your own, but you have to leave. You knew that, and now we're here to see that you do it."

After a pause, he added, "I'm sorry about your dog."

"How can you let them do this?" Jake asked, jutting his jaw in the direction of the uniformed men.

"All them CCC boys is in cahoots with the businesses over to the Shenando. You know they just wrote this new law so as they could take our land... and you're helping them?"

The CCC men he gestured toward looked back with varying degrees of empathy and indifference. One of them smirked. As a public works employment scheme, the Civilian Conservation Corps attracted a cross-section of the unemployed.

"I'm sorry, Jake. It's the law," the deputy continued. "It's our job. You have to understand that. The appeals have run out," he said with finality, "and the President himself has given the go-ahead for the Park."

Gerald had heard talk of something called the Park, but that was away over in Thornton Gap, where folks were looking at a bulldozer parked by the road. What did that have to do with Fletcher Hollow?

The deputy let his words sink in for a moment.

"Now we're going to put your things on this truck and take them to Flint Hill, and I don't want any more trouble. You're no good to your family in jail and that's where you're headed if we can't do this thing peacefully." Looking at Ruby, he added, "And that goes for you, too, ma'am."

For the next hour, Gerald and Aidan watched from their separate hiding places as the men of the Civilian Conservation Corps carelessly piled the family's belongings on the back of the truck.

The senior deputy instructed the men to leave food and clothing on the porch before they boarded up the windows and doors. The injured deputy stood by, holding his weapon in his good hand, as his partner released the handcuffs on Gerald's father. Then, leaving the victims in silence, the intruders headed back down the mountain.

* * * * *

The day after Christmas, 1935, eight months after the Fletcher's eviction, the Commonwealth of Virginia officially transferred the land for Shenandoah National Park to the Federal Government.

The next day men from a newly formed unit of the United States Park Service returned to the vacant homestead and burned the house to the ground.

CHAPTER 1

MAY 1965

Memorial Day was the first big day of the year for visitors to Shenandoah National Park. By ten o'clock that morning cars were already backed up three or four deep at the Thornton Gap entrance.

"Hi, Folks. Welcome to the Park," David Weston said, smiling as he touched the rim of his Park Ranger's hat.

He bent to look into the station wagon with its family, a mongrel collie and the makings for a picnic.

"Are you just visiting for the day?"

"That's right," the driver replied. "We plan to drive a little while and then have a picnic."

"Great. A day pass for your car will be one dollar, but if you'd like a season pass, it's three dollars."

After a brief exchange with the woman next to him the driver said, "I guess we'll just take the day pass," and handed a five-dollar bill through the window. "Where would you suggest we go for a hike and a picnic, not too far from here?"

"Well, there's Skyland, about ten miles south," he replied. "It has a nice picnic area and a walking trail to the lookout on Stony

Man Mountain. Great view of the Shenandoah Valley from there. Or you can go another ten miles to Big Meadows where you'd have a choice of trails."

David didn't mention the trail they would pass on the way to Skyland that led to the eastern slope of the Pinnacle. He'd discovered the area, with its tributaries of the Hughes River, during one of his off-season hikes, and he fancied it as his own corner of the Park. He wasn't a recluse by nature but, as the preacher's son from a nearby Baptist congregation, it suited him to have someplace in his world where he wasn't under constant scrutiny.

He handed the driver his change, the day pass, and a map of Skyline Drive.

"Here you are, sir, and please remember not to leave any food or trash lying around your picnic site. We have bears in the Park that are always on the look-out for something to eat."

There was the predictable wave of oohs and ahhs from the back seat and then the driver's dutiful question, "Is that something we should be concerned about?"

"No, no, not all. Just keep your picnic site clean and if you do see a bear, don't approach it," David answered, reciting the official guidelines. "You'll be fine. And, of course, be sure to keep your dog on a leash."

He glimpsed gestures of impatience from the next car in line, so he concluded, "If you have any questions, there is a ranger stationed in each camping area. Have a great visit."

David had started his summer job with the Park Service before school let out, working Saturdays as an attendant at the entrance to the Park. The first morning his mother saw him wearing his Park Service uniform she couldn't help smiling. The flat-brimmed hat was cocked slightly to show his neatly trimmed straw-blond hair, and, in the shadow of the hat, his eyes were an even richer shade of blue than usual. His strong features, once loose and boyish, had come together with a coherence reserved for grown men. His muscular six-foot frame filled out the Park Service uniform and a man's arms swung below the neat cuffs of the short-sleeved shirt. When did that happen? she wondered as she wiped her hands on her ever-present apron.

At first, David had been self-conscious in the uniform and he took no comfort from his mother's admiration; that's just how mothers are. But then, his first day on the job he'd caught a couple of girls gazing at him from the back seat as their car passed his station. That was good for a few moments of swagger and from then on he wore the uniform with ease.

A '54 Chevy sat in the lot next to the Park entrance where David could keep an eye on it. Seventeen years old and he had his own car. Well, almost. The title was in his father's name because insurance was cheaper that way, but he didn't have to advertise that. Now, if he could just make the varsity football team, senior year would be looking pretty good.

David had also worked in the Park the previous year and, like all summer recruits, he had started in Maintenance, cleaning campsites, and clearing brush and windfall from the hiking trails. By mid-summer, he had been promoted to crew chief and when he called the Park Service office to ask about working again this year, they didn't even ask him to fill out an application form.

In hindsight, he was probably a safe bet. First-born in a family of five, he had been given regular chores by the time he was ten. By fifteen he was working evenings and weekends at his father's church or at one of his minor construction concerns. In the not-uncommon-coincidence of character and belief, his father, James, was a firm believer in the evils of idleness. However, his commitment to the church and lack of business sense kept the family living close to the edge. They had the necessities, but if David wanted anything beyond that, he had to pay for it himself.

Reluctantly, James had agreed to the summer job with the Park Service.

"If you're not helping me in the Lord's work," he insisted, "or doing some of my jobs so I can focus on the Lord's work, then you must make sure, in the very least, to honor Him in what you are doing."

He repeated the concession speech this year, adding, "And that includes having a strict budget."

First, of course, there would be tithes to the church: ten percent of his $68 per week, straight off the top. Then there were his school clothing account, the $10 he was to give his mother for household expenses while he was working, and his bible college savings account. That left $20 toward car insurance, gas and repairs and $10 a week for lunches and pocket money. His father said $10 a week was certainly more than he needed, but it would be OK provided he didn't flash it around.

The Chev was in good shape for its age. His father agreed that the few things it really needed, like a carburetor kit and some body filler in a couple of the worst rust spots, could be paid for out of his regular salary. He dismissed anything else as frivolous. The pay raise had come after the budget discussion and David figured that, over the course of the summer, it might be enough to pay for the seat covers he had seen in the Sears catalog and an eight-track tape player. It would be close, but he could already feel the soft leatherette trim of those seat covers and hear Roger Miller declaring him 'King of the Road'.

His father had ruled out university.

"They teach Darwinism," he'd said bluntly.

David showed real promise as a preacher and his father and the elders of the community had developed an expectation that he would follow his father into the ministry. James agreed that Bible college would be OK, provided it was a God-fearing school that taught the gospel. None of this ecumenism or other conjurings that lured churchgoers away from the fundamental truth of Christ crucified.

James had left school after grade nine to help support his family during the Depression so he had no formal theological training. He cherished his few well-worn books by stalwarts of the faith like C. H. Spurgeon, whose Godliness was beyond question, but he was suspicious of most theologians; wolves in sheep's clothing, he called them. James drew his faith and his sermons mainly from his own scripture reading and prayer. His devotion to the Word of God and to his congregation was beyond doubt and when he said, "God says it, I believe, that settles it," no one ever challenged the scriptural validity of his conclusion. He had a rich vocabulary for the evils of the flesh and the righteousness of God but, with this parochial experience, his range of sermon topics was narrow, and his illustrations were limited.

There was a growing feeling among some in the church that there might be more comfort in Pastor Williams' teaching, "if it could convey a little more of the richness of man's experience with God," as Mrs. Elkins put it one afternoon over tea with a few of the ladies.

Charles Ford, the high school shop teacher, expressed the view of others when he said, "Maybe some of the feelings that trouble people from time to time should be looked into a bit, rather than just being nipped in the bud as threats to righteousness."

Others, who weren't so eloquent but who still squirmed under James' flame-thrower sermons, were heard to say vaguely, "Times have changed."

But the deacons were loath to raise these concerns with the pastor. There was too much he already condemned as heresy and the seeds of dissension. The hope was that David would join the ministry; but do things differently. That he would get the formal training his father lacked, see some of the Lord's blessings else-where in the world, and then come home to pick up where Pastor Williams left off. Instead of being a lay preacher, David would become the Reverend Williams, ready to offer a wider variety of sermons on Sunday and more equipped to help people face life during the rest of the week.

And while it was never spoken of, the ladies felt that it wouldn't hurt to have a Reverend leading the flock when community social events came around and they had to mingle with women from the Trinity Episcopal Church. Class may have had no place in the doctrine of either church, but it was right at home in the pews.

Such were the thoughts that lay behind the fondness people had for David, and their hopes for him. Those hopes accounted for old Andrew Barnett's decision to give David the car, so he could collect kids for young people's meetings and Sunday school and travel to his speaking engagements without adding to the demands on James' old Buick.

And if the boy gets a bit of pride out of having the car, Barnett thought to himself, *where's the harm?*

The cars and the occupants in the line at the Park entrance varied as the morning wore on but the routine was the same. People were generally in good spirits; anticipation of the outdoors did that to them. Some of the repeat visitors were a little short with David, anxious to let him know that they knew the drill, so he had a Welcome Back mode that included handing the visitors a leaflet entitled 'What's New in the Park' and wishing them a pleas-ant visit. He reminded himself with relief that once the regular summer schedule started, he would be back on trails, with a crew and equipment of his own. Sweat and a few scrapes and bruises beat this any old time. After each car, he glanced lovingly at the Chevy in the parking lot.

He generally took no notice of the cars in line until they pulled up to his booth but, toward mid-day, the loud music and raucous laughter from one car caught his attention as it turned off Route 211 and entered his line. It was Jerry Fletcher and a bunch of the guys from school. Six or seven of them all packed into Jerry's '56 Fairlane. This lot never needed an excuse to party and the party usually included cars and beer. He forced himself to concentrate on the customers in the car in front of him, but he wasn't looking forward to the digs he knew would come when that gang pulled up.

Jerry Fletcher was stern-faced and looked straight ahead as he came to a stop at the booth.

"Hey, Guys," David said, seizing the initiative, "Going to storm the mountain?"

"Up yours," Jerry muttered, holding out a ten-dollar bill without looking up. "Season Pass."

David was used to ridicule and sarcasm from these guys, but the hostility in Jerry's voice this morning surprised him.

"You got it," he said as he took the money and proceeded to make change and assemble the standard information package. Maybe Jerry was just trying to hide the fact that he'd been drinking.

"Hey, Preacher Boy, where's your Bible?" Tom Carter called from the back seat, and a couple of the others laughed.

"It's over there in the car. I can get it on my break if you want to stick around."

"Go to hell," Carter said and looked away awkwardly as one of the other occupants jabbed him in the ribs.

Another voice from the far side of the car chipped in, "Hey, Big Shot Park Ranger. Gonna convert Smokey this year?"

David bent to hand Jerry his change, the pass, and the printed materials. Now, young Fletcher had no choice but to look up. He took the money and the pass and snarled, "You can keep the rest of that propaganda bullshit."

There was beer on his breath, but the eyes were sharp.

"Your call," David said. It may have been a lapse in judgment, but he decided not to report the booze. In a voice intended only for the front seat, he said, "Hey, Jerry, easy on the sauce, OK?"

"Fuck you," Fletcher replied, with more embarrassment than venom.

As the car started up the hill someone turned up the volume on the radio again and there was a round of cheers from the passengers. Arms appeared from all of the windows and hands began to slap the roof in time with the music. Whatever was bothering Jerry had apparently passed.

CHAPTER 2

The idea to go to the Park had come up thirty minutes earlier when Jerry Fletcher and the others were already into their third six-pack. The deputy sheriff had given them a long look as they drove past his parked cruiser on Route 211. Going someplace where he wouldn't hassle them seemed like a good idea.

It wasn't until they reached Thornton Gap and turned into the line to enter the Park that the plan collided with his feelings about the mountains. Jerry was the first generation of Fletchers born away from the mountains but the bittersweet memory of the family's home and their eviction was part of him. Suddenly, sharing that territory with a rowdy bunch from school was a distasteful prospect.

By the time he pulled away from David's kiosk, Jerry had settled on a solution. They would stay away from Fletcher Hollow, or anything on that side of the Ridge for that matter. They would go to a regular picnic area, right on Skyline Drive. The guys would have enough woods to piss in and lots of tourist ass to look at. They'd have to keep the beer drinking under wraps so he didn't get his season permit revoked but, hey, tough shit! They'd just have to live with that.

Jerry only knew about the eviction and about his Grandpa Jake from the stories his father had told over the years, some around home but most when they camped together in the mountains. He also knew his father best from those camping trips. At home Gerald was a typical father, working long hours at the shop, disciplining around the house, and introducing baseball and football with improvised games on the side lawn after work. But sitting at a campfire or leaning against a rock, drinking sparingly from a canteen, he was different. *It's like something wakes up in him when he's on the mountain,* Jerry once thought, years later, as he watched his father head off down a familiar path.

Grandpa Jake had died not long after the eviction, never having made the adjustment to life on a twenty-five-acre piece of ground in the resettlement area. Too many regulations and too much paperwork; rent to pay every month, and officials always sticking their nose in his business. He wasn't their favorite client, either. "Gnarly as a locust fence post," one had said, "and just as hard to work with."

There didn't seem to be anything Jake could just go and do without checking with a stranger in some office, nothing that could give back a sense of determining his own future. Nothing ever replaced the helplessness he had felt that day watching his possessions being hauled off the mountain on the back of that truck.

He spent more time drinking and would sit for long spells gazing at the mountains and rubbing his wrists. With the alcohol, he became useless as a provider, and Aidan had taken over putting food on the family table virtually since the eviction. What was once harsh discipline became naked violence as Jake lashed out at the family in his frustration. Ruby had kept increasingly to herself in fear and embarrassment. The kids had found excuses to stay outside or away from the house altogether.

In the end, it was a fight in the back of Homer's Bar and Grill in Flint Hill that killed Jake. The Sheriff said they were all drunk.

It was hard to know who had started it or what it was about, but it must have been quite a fight. Broken glass and boards littered the yard and blood smears stood out, black in the flashlight beams against the tall unpainted board fence that enclosed the space.

Jake had been lying unconscious in the damp darkness when the Sheriff arrived and the two hours they took to get him to the hospital in Warrenton didn't help his chances. Gerald said later he was sure the fight was over the mountains. Someone had probably referred to those no-account hillbillies once too often. As it was, Jake died alone in an intensive care ward thirty miles from the mountains he loved and far from the family who would have saved him if they had known how.

With Jake's death, the family's transition to life off the mountain could begin in earnest. They stayed on in the little frame house on Resettlement Road, and Aidan found work at the farm supply depot on the edge of Flint Hill. By road, it was about an hour's walk, but if the Wilson Branch wasn't carrying too much water he could cut through the back fields and be there in about twenty minutes. Either way, there were chores to do when he got home. Gerald went to school and did odd jobs evenings and weekends, and Ruby and Chloe tended a vegetable garden and took in laundry and sewing to earn extra house money.

They could talk about their daily lives now without fearing the drunkenness and the beatings. Gerald still missed the hand his mother used to rest on his shoulder when they had been back on the mountain, or the pat on his butt as he'd start up the ladder to the sleeping loft. No one could remember the last time Ruby had laughed but at least she didn't cry anymore.

When Aidan did have a day off, he would hitchhike to the mountains or catch a lift with Mr. Mowatt, the owner of the grocery store on Main Street. A couple of times a month Mr. Mowatt would leave before dawn to make a run to the Shenandoah

Valley. Everybody knew that the folks on that side of the Ridge, with their German heritage, made the best hams and cured meats and, like any grocer in these parts worth the name, Mowatt made sure to offer his customers the real thing. His exact source was, of course, a trade secret and most regulars knew better than to ask. That would be like asking someone to reveal their favorite place to look for morels in the spring. If anyone ever did ask where he got his meat, he would just say, "Oh, a fella I know a ways the other side of Woodstock."

But he was always happy to give Aidan a lift and drop him off at the Buck Hollow trailhead or the top of Thornton Gap.

"Tell your mother I'll take a dozen bunches of beets when they're ready," he'd say as he pulled over on the side of the road or, "You remind her now, that she promised me the first of the fall spinach."

Like Gerald, Aidan had watched the eviction from a hiding place and felt helpless, and like Gerald, those memories would never die, but unlike his younger brother, Aiden's hours of trekking back and forth across the mountain checking on the cattle had given him a degree of self-confidence, a sense of himself, which he could reclaim just by returning. As often as the older boy would allow, Gerald went with him, listening intently to Aidan's instructions and quickly learning the skills his brother could offer.

By the time he was fifteen, Gerald would go to the Park himself, often paying his sister to do his chores so he could stay a night or two in the mountains. During the remainder of his adolescence, he built a framework of skills and knowledge around the legacy of those early years, but nothing could dull the vivid flashes of anger when he remembered the eviction. He came to manhood with a simmering hatred for the people and the organizations that had uprooted his family.

Hunting was a side interest, but he usually carried a rifle, or a fishing rod, and he got game often enough that he had to worry about being stopped by the warden. Like as not, the contents of his car trunk would be incriminating.

With a couple of auto mechanics courses in high school and lots of practice keeping the family car on the road Gerald had managed to get a job in Harland's garage, right there in Flint Hill, and in 1958 he bought the business from old man Harland. Today Fletcher's was the biggest automotive service center in the county, with its own car and truck sales department and even a branch in the next county.

Gerald Fletcher was a good businessman and a good provider, who cared very much for his family. But, if love was something more than caring and giving, if that was the word for the stirring and the comfort that became one in him when he returned to the mountains, then they were the true love in his life, and he spent as much time there as business and family permitted.

He married Faith, a classmate from nearby Huntly, and added a couple of family picnics a year to his own mountain visits. Once in early summer, and then again in the fall, he would put Faith (and later young Jerry) into the car and make the climb to Thornton Gap. He saw to it, though, that these picnic trips were bright, cheerful events. They went to established picnic sites, they took short scenic hikes, and on the way home they would always stop at the general store in Sperryville for an ice cream cone. As Jerry grew older, he began to refer to the area as the Park but, like others who had been forced out of the mountains, Gerald would never use that term.

When Jerry turned eight, Gerald took him on his first overnight trip to the mountains. This time they left the car at the Meadow Springs trailhead and as they began the gentle eastward descent toward the shoulder of the mountain, Gerald promised his son some new sights.

"I'm going to take you to see where Grandpa Jake and Grandma Ruby used to live," he said, and thus began the visits to Fletcher Hollow during which Gerald gradually passed on the story of his family. Sometimes it took the form of a running conversation as they explored the old yard or barn site or walked along the path to the spring.

"Hey, what's this, Dad?" Jerry asked one day as he pulled a heavy rusted blade from the long grass.

"Oh, that's Grandpa Jake's old mattock. He used to dig roots with that or loosen big rocks when he was getting the garden ready in the spring."

Sometimes the story unfolded by their campfire after a meal of beans and cornbread. Jerry would poke at the fire with a stick as his father stared reflectively into the flames.

"We didn't need much money and it all came from the land," he'd say. "A couple hundred dollars was about all it took in a normal year."

"That's a lot of money," the youngster corrected.

"Yes, I guess it is," Gerald admitted with a smile. "Anyhow, Grandpa Jake and Uncle Aidan would cut down chestnut trees and strip the bark to sell to the tannery at Thornton Gap. They hauled the logs to the sawmill next to the tannery, and they either got a share of the lumber back in trade or they sold it to the sawmill owner for cash.

"Then in the fall, trucks would come across Route 211 from the Valley and stop to buy chestnuts at collection points along the road where people waited for them with their baskets and boxes of nuts." Gerald would pause, remembering the almost magical sound of those few coins jingling in his pocket as he had made his way back to Fletcher Hollow with his earnings.

From time to time he would lean forward in the flickering light to see if Jerry had fallen asleep but, while the youngster might be propped up on his arms or slumped back against a log, he was invariably wide-eyed and listening.

"How'd you get the chestnuts?"

"Well, there's an old saying," Gerald continued. "It takes three people to collect chestnuts: one to shake the tree, one to pick up the nuts, and one to drive the hogs off. And, I'll tell you, that wasn't far wrong. Messing with a razorback boar or an old sow with a litter was serious business."

"Did you ever get chased by a hog?" Jerry asked.

"Hell, yes! Oops! Don't tell your mother I said that."

"Nah-ah," Jerry promised as if doing so would implicate them both.

"Anyhow, once an old sow come out of a thicket at us and I was the closest to her. Lucky for me there was a low branch on the tree we were working under and I just managed to haul myself out of her way in time. Your Uncle Aidan picked up a dead branch and clobbered her good. She run off, but we could hear her fussing and fuming in the brush for an hour before she finally decided not to try for us again."

"I'd be scared if that happened to me," the youngster said in a hushed voice.

"I was plenty scared too," Gerald assured him. "Depending on where we were collecting, we'd either take the nuts to Thornton Gap or we'd carry them down Buck Hollow and wait by the side of the road for the truck to come.

"And then in the late fall any spare time we had was spent shelling walnuts that we would sell to the general store in Sperryville. I'd rather have done most anything than shell walnuts. Those shells are so hard they have to be hit with a hammer to get 'em open, but if you hit 'em too hard, or hit 'em in the wrong place, you get a shattered mess."

There was an amused chuckle from the shadows on the other side of the campfire.

"More than once I got a cut from the shell or hit my finger with the hammer." *Little boy's hands weren't made for that kind of work,* Gerald thought to himself as he watched Jerry poking cautiously at the fire with his stick. Nor were the kerosene lamps that lit the table for evening sessions, their faint and dancing light making a difficult job almost impossible. But he had done his share. Jake's brand of discipline had seen to that.

"Where was your school, Dad?" Jerry asked on another one of their visits.

"Down in Old Rag, over that way," Gerald answered, pointing toward the western base of Old Rag Mountain where the village had been in the days before the Park. "One room for all eight grades. It took us more than an hour to walk down and longer to get home."

Gerald remembered how tired he would get walking back up the mountain in the afternoons, trying to keep up with Aidan; and how glad he was on the days when Jake would decide that something that needed doing around the farm was more important than going to school.

"And what about church?" Jerry asked, continuing down a list of the compulsory elements of his young life under which he had already begun to chafe.

"My Uncle Jeb—that would be your Great Uncle Jeb—he was the traveling preacher in these parts. He didn't have a church, but he had his Bible. He walked from one hollow to another, holding services in a couple of different homes each Sunday, helping us all to understand the scriptures and mind them as best we could."

It took Gerald years and many visits to the homestead with his son to finally inject the full venom into his accounts of the eviction. When Jerry was about fifteen, his father summed up the event.

"It was a bad thing, what they did. And they could only do it 'cause they thought we were trash." Then, after a pause, he added, as if to himself, "We just couldn't fight 'em."

But most of the time during their trips together, Gerald focused on life in the mountains. As they walked along the old tracks, now marked 'Fire Trail - Official Vehicles Only', he would point out plant life to Jerry, things that were edible and how they used to be cooked. He didn't know much about the medicinal plants, but he told a few stories that he'd heard from the old folks around the resettlement. He taught Jerry to hunt, to set traps, build a deer stand, call turkey, and track bear.

Gerald didn't see any problem with the fact that they hunted in a National Park, or that they hunted out of season; to him, these were just bureaucratic trappings of an administration that had lost its legitimacy the day it stole his family's way of life. They had to be smart and they had to be good, but he and his son were just taking back a token of what they had lost.

The result of this careful juggling of Jerry's education was an anger at what happened to his family that could be triggered in him on a moment's notice. The mere mention of the Park Service or the Government was enough. But he also came to love the mountains and to know them separate from the family history.

He and his father often camped in the yard of the old house, now marked only by the stone chimney and the hearth that they used on those occasions for their campfire. The smoke was just as likely to leak out a crack and drift up the outside of the chimney as it was to rise through the flue, but the biscuits cooked fine either way. As night deepened, the echoes of that fateful day would gradually diminish, to be replaced by the call of owls or whip-poor-wills and, by the time Orion slipped out of sight over the Ridge and the Big Dipper had swung in to hang overhead, they would both be sleeping soundly.

CHAPTER 3

Sounds pretty good, David thought, adjusting the volume on the eight-track tape player as he pulled into the school parking lot on the first day of class. It was too bad he could only afford two tapes. The Statler Brothers 'All-Time Gospel Favorites' sat on the seat beside him, ready for shuttling kids to and from church or if a church elder stuck his head in the window to admire the car.

"Good old boys from Staunton," Deacon Rogers had said when he saw the cartridge. "I know the Reid boys' father. Good church folks, they are."

But the Roger Miller 8-track was in the tape deck. It had enough music to get David most anywhere he needed to go without replaying a single song. Once classes got started, he'd see about borrowing or trading cartridges to get some variety of music. With the windows down, Miller's sound began to turn heads as the Chevy approached a bunch of the senior guys standing by the side entrance near the gym. Wisps of smoke rose defiantly from the group.

"Hey! Check out the wheels on the preacher," Billy Atkins said as he recognized David. Cigarettes were tossed to the ground as David passed, to be extinguished with exaggerated heel twists as Billy and the others moved toward the student parking area to inspect the new addition.

Cars were a sure draw. Whatever their self-declared lifestyles, every male fifteen and over saw cars in his future. The rednecks took auto shop and planned their lives around stock cars and the Dixie Circuit schedule. The jocks talked muscle cars and chopped-and-cuts. Cool dudes were into two-tone paint jobs, chrome hubcaps and plush velour seat covers in anticipation of that Saturday night when they would go all the way with their chick in the back seat. There were hippies who called cars chariots, and judged each one in terms of its ability to get them to California. The guys that began to make their way to where David was parking were all members of the Mechanics Club—rednecks and jocks.

David backed his car into an empty spot and the others walked up just as he was stepping out, quickly pulling at one corner of the new seat covers. He had put them on a few days before and they had fit just fine once he had drawn the straps together under the seat with a few paper clips, but he didn't want to chance a wrinkle.

"Not bad, David, my boy. Not bad." It was Hack Dodson, a ringleader among the auto shop gang. He was renowned for his capacity to launch enormous lugies from the base of his throat in a gesture repugnant to all but his peers, and the name had stuck, partly because Dodson allowed it to. He was a strapping five-foot-ten with the jaw of a cartoon muscle man, but his mother had christened him Harold. Hell, clarinet players were named Harold, not mechanics. "Ought to get you to church a few times," he continued with a chuckle, "provided you take it real easy."

"Yeah, sure," David retorted to cover the awkwardness he always felt around these guys, and then he did something he had promised himself he wouldn't do this year. He rose to the bait.

"I took a '60 Galaxy from the light in Culpeper the other day." Now he was in the comparison game, which he knew he would eventually lose. And worse, he had admitted to street dragging.

"Yeah, yeah, and what was the little old lady wearing?" It was Billy again.

"Had to be the 223 block," Steve Wolfe said. "The 272 would have blown you away." He was into the specs and stats of the car scene. Slighter of frame, he stood a little back from the leaders.

Then Roddie Jenkins caught on to the fact of the race itself.

"Hey! Hey! What's that you say? Did I hear the preacher say he was draggin'?"

A chorus of naughty-naughty followed.

"Well, it was all pretty innocent, actually," David explained. "I backed off at forty."

"Right, sure," said Jed Connolly. "And I pulled out the other night before I came." He was the only guy in school who still wore ducktails and, what's more, he thought he was setting a trend.

The banter was more good-natured than it might have been between this bunch of rough-and-readies and a preacher's son. They thought he was weird all right, with this bible stuff, but the car gave David some status and word had gotten around that he made the varsity football team. Of course, no one would admit to caring, but he was turning out to be more of an OK guy than they might have thought.

The football uniform he had taken home to be washed after the last preseason scrimmage was folded on the back seat. Next to it lay a couple of new notebooks and David's old King James Bible. The Bible didn't get equal billing in his vision for the year, but he couldn't leave it at home, either. His father would have hit the roof, but that wasn't the real issue. After seventeen years of Sunday school, church, and personal crises taken to the Lord in prayer, David couldn't step out of the pattern, even if he sometimes wondered about it. It would be like going to bed at night without saying his prayers. It wasn't his faith that was at issue; it was the ritual. But it didn't matter how much he discounted its importance during the day or how tired he was at night; he could not go to sleep without spending a few moments in a perfunctory recital at the side of his bed.

Once, he had made it into bed without saying his prayers, only to have to throw the covers back and slide out again; he imagined God chuckling at him.

Pastor Williams' official doctrine for high school students included the rule that they carry their Bible, on top of their books, to every class.

"You never know when one of your classmates will be convicted of their sin by the Holy Spirit, and you have to be ready," he would say when he participated in young people's meetings in the church basement. "How could you ever face Him if you hadn't been ready to help one of your classmates find Christ?"

No one ever complied fully with the rule, but David had carried his Bible enough over the last three years that everyone in school knew his stand and had come to take it for granted. So, as he opened the back door of the car and reached in to collect his things, the guys took note of the strange mix of items, but the football uniform balanced out the Bible, and the talk of cars hardly skipped a beat as it moved from David's wheels to the kind of general automotive facts and fantasies that served their social cohesion.

"Hey! D'you hear about this new stuff they got coming out? Supposed to make tires and dashboards look like new."

"Yeah, sure. Tell me another one."

"No, no. It's true. I seen it in Road and Track this month... Armor-something, they call it."

The halls were crowded as David entered the school and began to make his way toward his locker. He chuckled to himself as he saw the ninth-grade kids, stern-faced and worried, trying to read a floor plan and, at the same time, look as though they knew where they were going. Panic was only a moment away, held at bay by the even stronger fear of being humiliated if they dared show any sign of loss of control. David shook his head, amazed that three years had gone by since he had looked like that. Standing on the last step of the bus in front of the school that first morning, it had felt like he was on the edge of a cliff. *By Columbus Day,* he thought, *they'll all be cool cats.*

Seniors had their pick of lockers, provided they signed up before the first day of classes, and normally he would have chosen one near the parking lot and the gym (where most of the senior guys had theirs). But David had a reason to choose a locker further along the corridor. Her name was Sherry Atkins, and she and a couple of her friends had kept their old lockers near the entrance to the library.

Even a preacher's son who took his faith seriously couldn't make it to sixteen without trying a kiss or two, but Sherry was David's first serious relationship. They had been seeing each other for about a year, attending church and young people's events together, helping each other with their studies and, without admitting it even to themselves, beginning to discover first-hand the attraction between male and female anatomies.

When Sherry saw David approaching, her face lit with a smile that preempted any further conversation with her girlfriends.

"Well, hello there," she said, and they shared a discreet kiss before teasing by the other girls broke the momentary spell. David put a sweater and several books in his locker, selected a pen and notebook for class, then rejoined the group to await the homeroom warning bell.

Sherry was about five foot four so, as she leaned against him, she fitted perfectly under his arm. Her dark, medium-length hair was arranged in a modest bouffant and finished in a flip that bounced agreeably as she glanced up at him or chatted with the others. Her mother had insisted that sleeveless fashions weren't appropriate for school, so she wore a short-sleeved white blouse with her tartan skirt. The argument over the length of the skirt had gone more in her favor, so it stopped well above her knees. David was glad she wore bobby socks and saddle shoes instead of those weird, patterned tights that seemed to be showing up everywhere these days.

Bending toward her he whispered, "You look great," and was rewarded with a warm smile and a nudge.

The Atkins had lived in the county for generations and the home place, Aberdeen, sat on a low rise along the old highway, about a half-mile outside the village of Washington. David always felt intimidated when he visited Aberdeen, and it wasn't just the shyness of facing his girlfriend's family. There was wealth here, and tradition.

A long driveway climbed gently through well-groomed pastures, each with twenty or so of the Black Angus cattle that were Mr. Atkins' pride and joy. The house was a grand old antebellum structure, colonial brick, two stories, with a pillared porch running the full width of the front. With its slate roof and freshly painted white shutters, it filled the space among the surrounding oaks perfectly, and Mrs. Atkins always saw to it that there were banks of potted flowers at the top of the drive and around the porch. Beyond the house and a neat array of out-buildings, another two-hundred-acre patchwork of cornfields and pasture rolled away toward the base of Jenkins Mountain.

He had once heard his mother use the expression 'old money', and there was no more dramatic illustration of the term than to sit on the Atkins' porch on a summer afternoon, sipping lemonade from cut crystal glasses while Mrs. Atkins told stories about some of the more colorful branches of her family tree.

On one of David's early visits, Mr. Atkins had been telling a few tales of his own, more about the men who settled the county and started the farm.

To show his interest, David had interjected, "Well, sir, it sounds like your people have been in the county a long time."

"Oh, no, son," Atkins replied. "They didn't come until after the Civil War." Then, almost as an afterthought, he added, "But my wife's people have been here a long time."

Sherry, the oldest of the Atkins children, had two brothers and they were raised in traditional roles. It annoyed her that the boys were allowed to be messy around the house but it would never have occurred to her that running the vacuum every Saturday morning wasn't her job. Just like keeping the wood box by the stove full was theirs.

The line between man's and woman's work was just a fact of life. She wasn't beyond blurring that line from time to time, but it was never anything radical. Her mother thought it was unbecoming when she would take the pickup to town instead of the sedan to run errands but, when she saw her husband smiling with pride one day as his daughter headed down the lane in the old clunker, she decided that a touch of tomgirl could be overlooked in a good cause.

Sherry's vision of the future was not unlike the circumstances of her childhood. Perhaps on a farm, perhaps in a city somewhere, she would have her own family, her own home, and children to care for. Her man would be the head of the household. He'd provide for the family, make the decisions outside the home, and be home for dinner every evening. It was a Tide commercial and 'Father Knows Best' rolled into one, and she was fine with that. She'd seen how her mother managed to question, comment, sanction and reward her way to decisions she wanted, without the mantle of decision-maker. If she could do it, so could Sherry.

The warning bell sounded for homeroom and as they started to move toward class, David and Sherry kissed again. The first couple of times they had parted with a kiss, it was followed by some exchange like, "Have a good day," and "You, too," but in the shorthand of early intimacy, the gesture itself had become the wish.

The Reverend Billy Graham was one of Pastor Williams' approved theologians, and the church library had a copy of a recorded sermon by Graham in which he addressed issues faced by the Christian family. On the subject of teen romance, Graham cautioned parents, "Remember, Mom and Dad, it may be puppy love, but it's real to the puppy."

To Williams this was an example of the wonderful insights that distinguished Graham from run-of-the-mill preachers.

"Isn't it marvelous how God uses a man of faith to reveal His truth," he would say.

But listening to that sermon was the first time David resented a stalwart of the faith. He didn't doubt that Graham was a man of God, but the condescension toward young people in that sermon was out of line. He couldn't bring himself to voice his objection, but this was one of the first cracks in the armor of perfection that had always cloaked such figures.

In terms of locker-room scorecards, nothing noteworthy had happened between David and Sherry. They had become pretty good kissers, but the Holy Spirit had so far been able to insulate the rest of their anatomies. Oh, there was that one time when they were hugging, and David couldn't hide his erection. To his surprise and confusion, Sherry hadn't minded, and in fact, she had moved in against him in response to it. But neither of them said anything about it, then or after.

Chastity was right up there with carrying your Bible to class and, to reinforce it, there were a host of rules that fell just below the Ten Commandments. There was the Six-Inch rule, that stipulated the closest boys and girls could come to each other. There was the Always-Go-In-Group rule, and there was the Ten-P.M.-Curfew rule that was itself a rider to the Don't-Go-Out-After-Dinner-Unless-It's-To-A-Church-Function rule.

Even if he were to circumvent any of these limits, his behavior was constrained by two other issues. First, Sherry had started to attend young people's meetings and church with David; she was determined to live by the principles she was learning under Pastor Williams' ministry. That put David's behavior squarely on the line. And then there was the simple fact that he was awkward around girls. Afraid would be more to the point, but he would admit to awkward.

He liked being around girls. Their fragrance could mesmerize him, their touch would comfort him or put a twist in his gut. But he was always afraid of saying the wrong thing or behaving in a way that put them off. They somehow knew what was right in a given situation, so when they didn't respond to him the way he wished, it meant he was wrong. He put girls on a pedestal and drifted around its base in an emotional Never-Never Land, not knowing what he wanted or how to get it.

Whatever perpetuated this issue, David's mother had set the stage for it with her own emotional reserve. She was a caring, hard-working parent, but she almost never hugged her children or engaged in affectionate conversation with them. He remembered as a child watching other kids being hugged by their mothers and wondering what it felt like. In a preacher's wife, Ruth's behavior may have been seen as gracious reserve, but it meant that her own children didn't know the comfort of a mother's arms, and that void had gradually been filled with doubt and insecurity.

David struggled with two possible explanations: His mother didn't show him affection either because he didn't deserve it or because it was wrong to want it in the first place. In the religious paradigm of the Williams household, feelings like that took on moral significance, so even the most modest of his quests for attention from girls was accompanied by a vague sense of guilt.

Girls were friendly but remote, captivating but unknowable. His fantasies weren't of sexual conquest but of a longing for acceptance. They were built on deference, on supplication that grew until, following some imagined trauma, his fantasy girl would agree to hold him and comfort him, and that embrace would carry him into sleep.

As he grew older the fantasy took on more and more sexual content but even in the hottest moments of erotic imaginings, he could never have thought of aggression; intercourse was the ultimate expression of a woman's acceptance.

"Baptists are quick to point out that it's wrong for Catholics to deify Mary," David's Uncle Marvin had said. "There's no basis for it in scripture and praying to the Holy Mother is the same as worshiping a false god. But Baptists do exactly the same thing with women. Somewhere between purity and wisdom, they give a stature to women that puts them out of reach. Mind you, after they're married, Baptist women suffer just as much neglect and abuse as the next bunch."

Uncle Marvin was the black sheep of the Williams family and among his alleged transgressions were some that included first-hand experience with the opposite sex. Following a modest career in the Foreign Service, Marvin had retired early to a small farm in nearby Orange County. One Saturday morning during the previous summer David had traveled with him on a cattle run to Richmond. As usual, when he had an audience, Marvin held forth on a number of topics as they traveled and that day the main subject had been women and the church.

"Since Mary and Joseph were the last two to have a child without it, Baptists know sex is OK for procreation," he said, warming to his subject. "But the problem is how to justify sex when carnal pleasure is such an abomination."

The word sex was never uttered in David's family and he hoped that Marvin didn't notice the flush he felt on his ears.

"So, what do Baptists do?" Marvin continued, "They isolate that part of life and that part of a woman's anatomy. They cloak them in mystery and give them a spiritual aura. They surround women with such a veil of sanctity that half the members of the congregation become Holy Mothers, present or future. Hell, if that's how you think about women you might as well come clean and pray outright to one of them."

Marvin was getting more and more worked up as he spoke,

"Sex is OK if you pray before and after and promise not to enjoy it. What a crock."

By then David was sure his ears were red, his whole face for that matter.

"Look at the damned ignorance of it," Marvin continued. "Not only do good-little-boys buy something for life without even knowing if it'll fit, but they have no clue what to do with it if it does. And God help the girl who might have the experience to remedy the situation."

Marvin was so into his subject that he hardly skipped a beat as he downshifted and pulled into the roadside café where they usually stopped for coffee and a piece of pie.

"So, for guys and girls both, the forbidden fruit ripens in fantasy. It gets further and further from the simple reality of male and female and pleasure and comfort."

Once again, Marvin had challenged him with ideas that couldn't be repeated but neither could they be forgotten.

* * * * *

"Good Morning, ladies and gentlemen."

The PA system came to life about ten minutes after the home-room bell sounded. It wasn't the announcement that got everyone's attention but the sarcasm of the sing-song response of the class: "Good morning, Dr. Winfrey."

Mrs. Burford allowed a wave of groans and eye rolls to run its course.

"My name is Dr. Winfrey, and as the principal of Rappahannock County High School it is my pleasure to welcome you for the academic year 1965–1966. If this is your first year here, you may be finding everything a bit overwhelming, but I want to assure you that your teachers and your upper classmates will give you all the help you need to feel at home."

David grunted almost involuntarily, remembering the kind of help his upper classmates gave him that first year. Like pouring lighter fluid under the bathroom stall door and lighting it. He had just had enough time to jump onto the seat before the flame reached the base of the toilet. Fortunately, their timing wasn't as bad as it could have been, and all he had to contend with was a wet spot on his pants for the first period after lunch.

The principal continued, "I trust that those of you in the middle years have returned with a resolve to build on your experiences and bring even greater maturity to the opportunities that wait for you this year."

"What crap," someone mumbled from the back of the room, and Mrs. Burford had to tap her pen firmly on the desk to restore order.

"And to those of you in your final year with us, let me just say, don't start celebrating too soon."

A chorus of exaggerated "Awe, shucks" rose from the class.

"You still have a lot of work to do but it is a year to celebrate endings and new beginnings, and we on the faculty look forward to sharing some of those celebrations with you.

"One important note for the gentlemen of the senior class," Winfrey continued. "There will be a special meeting with a representative of the Selective Service Board during second and third periods next Thursday. Your attendance is required."

The principal went on to announce various club activities but David and the other guys in the senior class were no longer paying attention. Each was once again confronting the incongruity of everyday life as a draft-age male in a time of war.

This had all been brought into sharp relief that summer with the Gulf of Tonkin incident. President Johnson's rhetoric was all peace and the Great Society but expressions like troop build-up, taking the offensive, and escalation kept turning up in the media. What they all boiled down to was that now there was a very real chance that the next stop for these guys would be military service and, for some of them, combat. Jobs and cars and girlfriends would be going on hold.

For the most part these were country boys, familiar with life outdoors, physical work and firearms. Some of them even got a kick out of fantasizing about a role in the conflict. 'Gonna kill me a commie gook' had a satisfying ring to it, and it got a lot of play in the banter among some of the jocks and rednecks. But such a fantasy was short-lived for anyone who actually thought about it. Hell, maybe the commie gook will get me first. Maybe I'll come home without a leg or, worst of all, with my balls blown off. A guy might as well be dead.

So, there were a few pistol and rifle gestures following Winfrey's announcement but, for the most part, the room was silent. David exchanged glances with two people. The first was Sherry, seated beside him in the next row, with an expression of dark concern. The second, just beyond her toward the windows, was Jerry Fletcher. They hadn't seen each other since the strained encounter at the Park entrance three months earlier. David had no reason to expect anything but a continuation of that hostility.

Instead, Fletcher just shrugged and, with almost a smile, said, "So what would you expect? It's the Government."

CHAPTER 4

Jerry had no interest in college. He was learning the automotive business working evenings and weekends with his father and he was comfortable with his parents' assumption that when he finished high school he would work in the garage or in sales and eventually take over the business. He would enjoy his time with the guys and stay within sight of the mountains.

He didn't fancy going anywhere or seeing anything that he couldn't get to with a few days off—maybe a weekend in Atlantic City or a trip to Nashville. One day he would probably drive to Florida just to see it, but there was no hurry for that. When the time came, he would marry, but he had already rehearsed the speech to his wife, whoever she would be, that marriage and family life weren't going to interfere with his time in the mountains. He loved his time there. He hunted. He fished. He had a regular buyer for any game he took, and it provided him with a very good income for a high school student. He certainly wouldn't have to start a savings program if he wanted a tape player or seat covers for his car.

His outdoor skills included equal parts hunting and eluding the law. Both were, in fact, a game that generated the adrenaline his peers might have experienced on a football field. Avoiding rangers and game wardens had led to him becoming familiar with the full length and breadth of the Park instead of just the area closer to home. By using different cars from the family business and different entry points around the Park's three-hundred-mile perimeter, he could avoid establishing a detectable pattern. He limited his chances of being recognized and he had enough parking places for vehicles that even if one were noticed from time to time, it wouldn't attract attention.

Only rarely did he actually conceal his car. If it was ever discovered there would be no simple way to explain the effort of hiding it. So, if he left a vehicle in the Park it was always at a trailhead or campground, with necessary permits clearly displayed. Around the perimeter, he made it look like a hiker's vehicle, leaving a knapsack or a change of shoes in full view. A couple of times, when he needed transport at a particular location because his prize was too heavy or obvious for a long haul, he left the car on the side of the road with a flag, as though it were disabled, only returning to it when he had everything within reach for a quick load and departure under cover of darkness.

Jerry didn't disclose his poaching activities to any of his friends. Serious poachers worked in teams of two or three, but he wasn't into it big-time. He didn't need the help and he didn't want the added risk. Besides, having someone other than family with him would break the connection he felt when he was in the mountains.

As far as his friends were concerned, he had a loner streak. It was weird that a guy spent so much time in the mountains, but they didn't care as long as he was his usual generous self when he was with them. They just assumed that the car and truck business must be pretty good since he always had money for gas and an extra six-pack.

The final part of his strategy was to enter the Park at Thornton Gap once every couple of months using the same car he drove to school and spending an afternoon or an overnight in innocent enjoyment of a couple of nearby trails. Without overdoing it, he would visit with one of the rangers and talk about some recent weather event or an ongoing project such as trail improvements. The rangers would recognize him and talk among themselves afterward about how he was the son of one of the former residents and how good it was that he came back to the Park so often.

While he might not have realized it, this immediate concern about the gamekeepers kept a sharp edge on his hatred of government at large. More than once he would put a ranger or warden in the crosshairs of his rifle scope as he hid on a ledge waiting to descend out of the Park with his game. Chances were that he would recognize the person wearing the uniform, a local resident or somebody's neighbor, so the fantasy of pulling the trigger never went beyond a power trip. But the image of the uniform caught in his sights stayed with him, and he could invoke it at any time.

* * * * *

"But if you don't go to college, you'll get drafted."

Once again, Connie Burke was trying for Jerry's attention as they sat opposite each other in the cafeteria.

"Two years in the Army is two years less wasted than going to college," he replied.

His matter-of-fact tone had as much to do with his lack of interest in Connie as with his lack of concern about military service. *It might even be interesting to learn some of the tactical stuff,* he thought. *Get to know bigger caliber weapons.*

Stories of boot camp and life in the field certainly didn't intimidate him, but he would never volunteer. He hated the idea of being labeled as serving his country. Joining the Army would in some way betray those who had lost so much, but if he were drafted, he would have no choice. As long as he didn't volunteer for anything once he was in, he thought the family would be okay with it.

He would have been completely happy with the future that was shaping up for him in the family business were it not for one nagging little hitch. Few of his teachers ever took note of the ease with which he did what was needed to pass, nor did they push him beyond the level of rote and learned behavior that signaled the progress of the class as a whole. But his math teacher in grades 10 and 11, Leslie Hanby, had noticed. When he called on Jerry, his answers were always camouflaged in an off-the-cuff style, but he was quick with mental arithmetic. More than that, the logic in his approach to problem solving reflected a capacity for deduction and synthesis that Hanby found remarkable. When he challenged Jerry or asked him to elaborate on how he had come up with his response, the lights would come on and there was definitely somebody home.

During these exchanges there would be mumbling undercurrents among his cronies; they would shift uneasily and wait for the chance after class to joke and poke, to reassure themselves that good old Jerry hadn't turned serious. Jerry always felt uncomfortable after such an episode, not because of his cronies (he didn't care what they thought) but because he saw glimpses of a part of himself that had no place in the future he had planned.

In a small school like Rappahannock High, the role of guidance counselor rotated among teachers on a yearly basis and Mr. Hanby was Jerry's guidance counselor in Grade 12.

SAT's were given that fall and follow-up was part of the guidance counselor's duties. Jerry didn't see any value to the tests in light of his own plans, and he had treated the whole process in the same perfunctory manner he used for term papers and other assignments. When his turn came to discuss the SAT results with Mr.

Hanby in the Guidance Office, the only thing on his mind was whether the meeting might drag on past the change-of-period bell. He had a set of brakes to turn in auto shop that afternoon and it would take the full period to get them done.

"Come on in, Jerry," Hanby said. "Take a seat."

The room was small, adding to Jerry's vague discomfort as he sat in front of the desk. "How are things going for you this year?"

"OK," Jerry replied, his tone non-committal. He had no reason to be hostile toward Mr. Hanby, but neither did he feel any obligation to respond to such a conventional icebreaker.

"Are there any subjects causing you difficulty?"

"No, sir. Under control." Then he thought of a way to put the ball back in Hanby's court and added, "Unless you know something I don't."

"Not at all," Hanby replied with an assuring tone. "In fact, that's just what I've been wanting to talk to you about. Let's start by getting these SAT results on the table."

He pulled the top sheet of paper from a stack in the desk drawer and glanced at it as though to verify the results he had read a dozen times. Then he looked at Jerry with a smile.

"Your score on the SAT was 1410, Jerry. That puts you in the top 5% of students who took the test in the whole country."

Hanby let his statement sink in for a moment, hoping that the enthusiasm he felt was contagious. But, other than an awkward smile, Jerry had no reaction.

"What's even more impressive," he continued, "is that you did equally well on the verbal and the math parts of the test. You excelled in both. Congratulations!"

Still only a modest "Thanks" from Jerry.

"Does this surprise you?" Hanby asked.

"Yeah, sure. I don't think about stuff like that usually."

Hanby took a different tack.

"Well, now that you have these results in front of you, what do you think?"

"I guess they mean that I should be OK in understanding things and in solving problems."

Whether it was out of frustration or a change of tactic, Hanby leaned forward and locked Jerry's eyes with his own.

"Look, Jerry. Let's cut to the chase. These results mean that you have the ability to take on just about any field of study you choose. You can have pretty much any career you want." He left that conclusion to settle in for a moment and then added, as if to address the first objection he anticipated. "And they mean that you can probably get a full college scholarship if you bring your grades into line with your ability."

"Well, that's all very interesting, sir, but I've decided to stay with the family business."

"And I certainly don't want to suggest that you shouldn't," Hanby reassured him. He had no interest in being the subject of an angry outburst in a PTA meeting. Who the hell is this guy, putting down what we do for a living?

"It's just that you need to know that you have choices," he said, "And maybe that you have the chance to look at other things in life before you settle down to your career at the shop."

On the wall behind the small desk, there was a poster for a jazz festival, depicting a streetlamp on Bourbon Street. It was mounted behind a sheet of glass and, as Jerry's eyes rose in search of a change of subject, he didn't notice the subject of the poster but the reflection. Mount Marshall and the Blue Ridge were about five miles north of the school, and the strong early afternoon sunlight projected their reflection onto the glass with the clarity and contrast of an Ansel Adams photograph.

"Have you ever thought of travel, Jerry? Of seeing how people live in different places?"

"No, sir, not really. To be honest, I don't have much interest beyond the county. I'm looking at a pretty good career with the car and truck business. And then there's that," Jerry said, raising his head in the direction of the poster.

From where he sat, Hanby could not see the reflection and he was at a loss as to Jerry's reference.

"But you said you weren't interested in travel... what connection do you have to New Orleans?" he asked.

"No. No. Sorry, sir. There's a reflection of the mountains in the glass. That's what I was talking about," he said, pointing over his shoulder out the window. What he had hoped would be a subtle end to their discussion of his future had turned into awkward confusion.

Hanby nodded his understanding and after a few moments said, "Those mountains mean a lot to you. That's good. Our heritage is an important part of who we are. The only thing I'll say is that they will always be there."

Jerry's mind challenged that statement instantly with a reflection on the family's eviction, but he said nothing and Hanby continued. "It will never be easier than it is now for you to take some time to look around, maybe try something different."

When school let out, Jerry told the guys that he couldn't hang out tonight. Tommy Dodson announced that he would catch a lift home with him, but Jerry told him he wasn't going home. There was no way he would admit to them that he just wanted to be alone, so after several questions and suggestions, he finally said, "Look, just fuck off, all right?" and left them to shrug at each other as he headed for the parking lot.

He didn't care that he turned up stone from the school driveway as he accelerated onto the highway. The vice-principal was going to chew him out for sure, but that would be tomorrow.

He didn't go home but neither did he go to the mountains. In the aftermath of the conversation with Hanby, both seemed to be part of the problem. In fact, if he read Hanby right, the problem was anything he felt comfortable with. With no destination in mind, he turned off the highway at Ben Venue and headed toward Laurel Mills on the two-lane road that rose, turned and fell with the terrain.

Apparently, there was some rule that if you're intelligent you're supposed to throw everything you know out the window and do something different. Why? So you can get your name on some building or some mathematics principle? The Fletcher Building? The Fletcher Principle? *Here's a principle for you, Hanby: Fuck you!* He turned his anger loose with a menacing hiss and glared through the windshield as the car began to accelerate.

"Leave things alone," he growled, as the car approached a rise in the road. "Leave me alone."

The curve on the downside of that hill would have been demanding at 45 miles an hour; at 65 it was close to impossible. As the car topped the rise the feeling of weightlessness suddenly grabbed Jerry's attention and he was focused on driving again before the full weight of the vehicle settled back onto its wheels. It teetered on the edge of rolling as friction in the screeching tires fought centrifugal force to complete the turn, but he found and held just the right mix and, with a bit of luck, brought the vehicle back under control. Coasting another hundred yards he stopped by the small bridge over Battle Run, turned the key off, and sat without moving.

As the adrenaline subsided, his anger with Mr. Hanby returned and he pounded the steering wheel with a fist.

"This is fucking ridiculous," he said, throwing the car door open.

Raising the trunk lid, he reached into a box under a canvas tarp, pulled out a mason jar and spun the top off.

"Here's to you, Hanby, you son of a bitch." He saluted with the jar in the direction of the school and then downed a generous portion of the moonshine.

CHAPTER 5

Football in junior year had been David's first experience with organized sports, so making the final cut for the varsity team the following year was no mean feat. But, as a friend of his would say years later, "Good boys have one thing going for them: they know how to please."

When the the coach barked "Belly bump!" David was the first one to hit the ground. When the coach said, "I want to see some hitting out there," David gave it to him. So much so that after practice one night a couple of the guys had a few choice words for him to take home and think about. But when, in a fit of frustration toward the end of a lackluster practice, the coach said, "OK. Nobody goes home 'til I see some blood," those same guys had been glad to have David on their squad.

Of course, it didn't hurt his performance that he weighed two hundred and ten pounds or that he had spent the two months before training camp wielding an ax and a chain saw for the Park Service. He carried much of his weight in broad shoulders and in muscular legs that were a good two inches shorter than most other six-footers. That gave him an advantage in starting, turning, and stopping, and that quickness had earned him his slot as a cornerback.

"Holy Shit! D'you see that?" Tom Carter asked as some of the shop guys watched the team practice one afternoon from the grandstand. "He come off the line like he was burnin' nitro!"

After that, David was as likely to be greeted in the halls with "Hey, Nitro" as with any reference to his faith.

Football became his ticket to social acceptance without having to compromise his stand on Christianity. Unlike nearly everything else high school kids did for entertainment, football was not explicitly banned by Pastor Williams and other faith leaders who shared his doctrine.

"Dancing is the vertical expression of horizontal desire," Bill Jamison had said during chapel hour at camp a couple of summers earlier. He was one of several evangelists scheduled through the church community on a regular basis because of their special ability to reach young people.

The movies and Hollywood frequently came in for vilification.

"But what about 'The Ten Commandments'?" a friend of Sherry's had asked. Not only was it a movie about the Bible, she argued, but it was old enough to be a classic. Everyone in the chapel tent had some version of the same question: What's wrong with Born Free? What about the Nutcracker Suite? What about Bambi?

"There may be some good in some parts of some movies," Jamison had answered, and then summarized, with one of his catchy phrases. "But you would be just as well off looking for a meal in a garbage can. The chances are too poor and the risks are too great." He was on a roll, so he added, "And don't forget, when you buy a movie ticket you're supporting the evil that is Hollywood, whatever the movie might be."

Playing cards wasn't a big pass-time among David's classmates, but it was taboo because of the superstitions that surrounded the figures in the deck and because cards were associated with gambling.

"But when the old folks play hearts at the rest home are they sinning?"

"The Bible doesn't say only to avoid evil," Bill explained. "It says to avoid the appearance of evil. Playing cards has the appearance of evil. Coming out of a movie theater has the appearance of evil. You have to think not only about what is evil in and of itself, but about what might appear to be wrong to someone who may be influenced by how you live your life."

Even bowling and shooting pool were on the list, having to do with the unsavory characters one was likely to meet in bowling alleys and pool halls.

Of course, drinking, smoking, and gambling were hardcore—right up there with killing and coveting. If you were found in any of those activities you became the subject of the most fervent prayers for an act of God's grace, and anyone who found Christ or returned to Him from such depths of iniquity would be a star attraction on the testimony circuit for months afterward.

David had his moments of doubt on some aspects of this doctrine but, for the most part, he believed it and he adhered to it. He didn't miss any particular activity, if for no other reason than that he didn't know what he was missing, but he did have a general feeling of being left out. He longed to be part of the camaraderie when a bunch of the guys headed off after practice. *It's almost like if it's fun, it's wrong,* he thought on one of the drives home alone after declining another invite to hang out with the guys back of the Sperryville General Store.

It didn't bother him that his parents showed no interest in his after-school activities. They had a lot on their minds, he told himself, including his four siblings; during twelve years of schooling, he had never known them to attend anything but parent-teacher conferences. Still, it would be nice to have them come to a game sometime and he decided to propose it.

His father worked hard in his construction business, but he was not well organized. His scattered work habits and last-minute commitments added to the time work demanded and often left his chair empty at mealtime.

Sunday was different. The mid-day meal was a sit-down affair after church, over which he presided. It began in a rather solemn state because the family was expected to be reflecting on his sermon that morning, but one or two questions or thoughtful comments were usually enough to reassure him as to the quality of his message and the spiritual health of his family. Even the youngest children had learned to wait out this stage politely and, by the time the gravy had been thoroughly mushed into the potatoes and the peas neatly arranged to one side of the carrots, the conversation could once again warm to the medley of topics and speakers that is confusion to an outsider but the essence of family to a member.

"Hey, Dad," David chipped in one Sunday in late September, as though he had just thought of it, "Coach moved me up to first string this week. I get to start against Warrenton Friday night."

James hesitated a moment and then said, "That's pretty good, I guess."

David realized by the tone that he had opened an old door. There was no way he could close it now, so he sat and waited until James continued, "... although I'd be happier to see you spending your energy on something else. You know the Apostle Paul said, 'Bodily exercise profiteth little.'"

David remained silent. Inviting his parents to the game no longer seemed like the best idea he'd had that day.

"But if the Lord has put you on that team to minister to those boys," James continued, "just see that you use every opportunity to do so."

"Of course, Dad." David responded reassuringly. It wasn't beyond the realm of possibility that his father would forbid any

further football playing. "The other night after practice I was sing-
ing 'Onward Christian Soldiers' in the showers." Even as he spoke,
he felt as silly reporting the gesture as he had performing it.

The locker room was David's least favorite part of football. The
other guys were at their bawdiest while he was at his most self-conscious. They strutted and swaggered with seeming indifference to
their genitals, when in fact the posturing showed their endowments
to advantage. David was reasonably equipped but it would be years
before he would realize it because in the locker room Nature read
his self-consciousness as a danger signal and withdrew to a protec-
tive posture in direct contrast to the confidence on display around
him.

Then there was the conversation, if that's what it could be
called, the exaggerated reports of conquests past and pending and
detailed descriptions of the anatomy of various cheerleaders and
campus sweethearts. Some of the images would stay with him, to
become the stuff of fantasy when he was alone, but acknowledging such thoughts to others, even with a nod or a smile, was so alien
that he would blush even at the prospect.

One night after practice, as the members of the team were in
various stages of undress and redress, Jeff Corbin confronted David.

"Hey, Preacher Boy, what about you. Do you screw or is sex a
sin, too?"

Despite the heat that flared around his ears at being singled out
on the subject, David responded with what he understood to be the
correct answer. "Sex is OK for making children."

A collective guffaw echoed about the room as his answer was
repeated down the rows of lockers, and bursts of laughter continued to highlight the fading banter until the last of the team had
made its way to the parking lot.

He couldn't have provided more entertainment for these guys
if he tried. But, beyond the embarrassment of it all, he knew there

was something out of line in what he had said. It may have been right in terms of what he heard from the pulpit, but it didn't square with how he felt—sometimes horny, sure, but even then there was something else, a longing for something, a need for the warmth and comfort that, somehow, being close to a girl would provide. Something was missing without it and, when his imagination overcame his self-consciousness, how right it felt when he pictured himself in Sherry's arms.

OK, jacking off was a sin, but there was no way that something as constant as sexual awareness, something so closely linked with comfort and affection, could be only for reproduction. A quick poke in the dark every year or two would suffice for that. Somewhere between moral tirades from the pulpit and vulgarities in the locker room there was something of value, something of importance, but what was it? Nothing in his life so far—church doctrine, parents or peers—had offered a premise he could trust to go looking for it.

He sat in his car in the student parking lot and watched absentmindedly as the last of the other taillights pulled onto the highway and faded in the distance.

Later that evening the telephone rang in the Williams home and he heard his father pick up the receiver. After a couple of minutes of conversation with the person on the line, James called up the stairs.

"It's for you, David. Your Uncle Marvin."

"Hey, Uncle Marvin," David said as he reached the bottom step and took the receiver from his father. "It's been a while."

"Yeah. How've you been, kid?"

"Not too bad, I guess. What's up?"

"Well, I was hoping you might be free to give me a hand this weekend. I want to take a load of feeder calves to the Winchester sale and my usual helper isn't available."

David's only concern was how to control his enthusiasm. Black sheep or not, Marvin was a breath of fresh air and tonight he felt like he was suffocating. He couldn't imagine a better fix than a day in no-holds-barred conversation with his uncle.

"Yeah, sure," he said. "Just let me check with Dad in case he has something planned for me."

"I've already run it past him," Marvin commented, "but that'd be good style just the same."

When he went into his father's office to ask if he needed his help this weekend, James raised a hand partway through the request.

"No, it's fine," he said.

David managed to contain his delight to the extent of only whispering "Yes!" as he headed back down the hall. He agreed to be at the farm by six o'clock Saturday morning and returned to his room with more enthusiasm for his lot in life than he had felt all day.

James couldn't help but detect the happiness in his son's voice. As the phone was returned to its cradle in the hall, he was once again left to reflect on the closest thing to a dilemma that his sense of conviction could accommodate. His younger brother, Marvin, had rejected the teachings of the church, and his anecdotes and attitudes told of a life lived well beyond the guidance of scripture, certainly as James read it. That was grounds to limit David's exposure to Marvin.

But he also sensed that his own strict worldview could, one day, push David to outright rebellion. He bore the God-given responsibility to steer his children away from that danger. So, letting David spend time with Marvin was risky, but it was a risk worth taking to give the boy a look at the things of the world while he was still living under James' roof. He would have preferred the clarity of adhering to a good Old Testament order, but there was a degree of realism here that gave him some comfort each time he confronted the issue.

But none of this occurred to David. All he knew was that he would be spending time this weekend with someone whose views and experiences were different from those he'd been raised with, someone who could give him a new take on what his future might look like. The sacrilege of considering Marvin's telephone call a gift from heaven didn't escape him but, nevertheless, when he whispered, 'Thank you, Lord,' he meant it.

* * * * *

The Angus calves were nervous at being herded and penned in the early dawn light. At five hundred pounds each, there was nothing calf-like about them when one would suddenly bolt in the direction of its captors in an attempt to return to the fields it knew. On a previous occasion, David had been sent flying by one of the calves and was lucky not to have been seriously hurt. Marvin had taught him that slow and steady was the order of the day when moving cattle, using the stout cane mainly as an extension of his arms. But one lasting effect of that encounter was that he was much less reluctant to give a would-be-escapee a good smack with that cane to turn the animal back.

By seven o'clock they had the calves loaded into the stock trailer and were ready to head for Winchester. The first order of business, however, was a stop at the cafe on the edge of Orange. David went in to buy coffee and sausage-and-egg biscuits while Marvin waited in the truck, ready to move the trailer a few feet as a distraction if the calves got restless.

"There should be a couple plastic cup holders in there," Marvin said, pointing to the glove compartment as David got back in the truck. "Maybe someday truck makers will wake up and build cup holders into the dash."

In short order the coffees were seated in their holders, hooked to each door, and the wrapping had been folded back on the breakfast biscuits. Holding his biscuit and the steering wheel in his left hand, Marvin started through the gears and the truck and trailer pulled gently out onto Route 15 and accelerated.

"Winchester, here we come," he said and took the first bite of his biscuit.

The heater gradually took the chill out of the cab and a sense of well-being settled into the space. They traveled in silence at first, enjoying their breakfast, with Marvin glancing routinely at the side-view mirrors. After several minutes he said,

"I guess everybody's settled down back there. The trailer's not rocking."

"Yeah, I don't feel anything either," David replied.

"Kate sure knows how to make a breakfast biscuit," Marvin continued, as he shoved the now-empty wrapper into the bag on the seat between them.

"For sure," David agreed, downing the last of his biscuit.

"So, did you have a hot date last night?" Marvin asked, with a twinkle in his eye.

"Yeah, right," David said dismissively.

"Come on! A good-looking stud like you? Varsity football team, senior class. I bet the women are lining up."

"No. Wrong guy. This is the local preacher's son, remember? Trying to follow the rules."

"But, unless you're trying to become the first Baptist monk, why can't you be both?"

"Come on, Marvin. You know that's not possible."

"Well, maybe you need to take a look at the rules, then. Who made them and why?"

"God made them," David said matter-of-factly.

"Don't give me that crap." David flinched but didn't say anything and Marvin continued. "First, even Bible thumpers recognize that God spoke through human authors. If you want to say that the scriptures were written under divine guidance, OK; it would be a waste of time to debate that one way or the other. But second, unless you're into big-time stuff like murder or adultery, what we're talking about probably isn't even in scripture; it's in the rules men produced later based on their interpretation of scripture."

David looked at Marvin, his expression trying to cope with disagreement and curiosity at the same time. His uncle wouldn't be stupid enough to misquote scripture to him, would he? But this can't be.

"I don't know, that sounds like heresy to me," he said.

"No, no, it's true. For example, Let's just say for the sake of argument that we're talking about premarital sex," Marvin said, winking at David. "Not that that's of any particular interest to anyone we know. If ever there was a no-no hammered into young people, that would be it, right?"

David nodded, suddenly awkward.

"I picked up a brochure one time," Marvin continued, "a tract that was left in the men's room by someone with a mission. The message was that sex outside of marriage was a sin and it listed eleven scripture references to prove it."

David was sure he knew at least half of them by heart, but he let Marvin continue.

"I looked them all up, just for the hell of it, and you know there was not one reference to premarital sex. The only specific acts ever mentioned were incest and adultery. Hell, even for the sicko that might think about incest, Mendel's work shows us how stupid that is. And adultery? Whatever else it might be, that's breaking a contract, breaking a promise." Marvin paused for a moment, then added, "OK, I may have broken a few promises in my time, but that's a different story.

"Every other reference in those verses," he continued, "was to something called fornication in the King James Version or sexual immorality in later versions.

"Right," David said, and that includes sex outside marriage."

"Says who?" Marvin countered. "The original Greek word that these bibles are working from translates to lewd or wanton behavior. That's a long way from two adults who care for each other making love."

David sat in silence, but his mind was racing. Could what Marvin was saying be true? Was there room for discretion in some of these things that had heretofore been banned? Sex? No, that would be too radical a change. There must be something wrong. But what if it's true?

Marvin was speaking again, "It makes perfectly good sense for a society to have rules against sex outside of marriage, especially a society based on the traditional family like ours, and especially when there was no such thing as effective birth control. But that's very different from God saying it's a sin."

"But in Mathew," David objected, "it says if anyone even looks at a woman with lust in his eye he has sinned."

"OK, but what's lust?" Marvin asked. "Here's another example of the church flipping something on its head: lust leads to sex, therefore sex is evidence of lust. Come on. Lust gets more skunks killed on the road in February than any other time of year. The poor bastards are so hung up on finding a lady friend that they ignore the traffic. But does that mean that every dead skunk on the road is proof of lust?"

David wanted to laugh but at the same time it annoyed him to be distracted from a serious issue.

"Lust is primeval," Marvin said, "a base instinct. It's getting your genes into the next generation and having a hormone high while you're at it, without giving a shit for the other person. It's all about taking, not caring or sharing. I'm OK with being opposed to that, for whatever reason, but I don't see what the hell it has to do with two adults who care for each other making love." He looked at David and concluded, "It was the rule-makers who decided to include premarital sex in those definitions, not God, and today's morality militia never questions it."

David was silent, and obviously processing what he had heard, so Marvin left him to it. He took the lid off his coffee, checked to see if it had cooled enough, and took a long sip. Sometimes he liked to hold forth purely to vent on a subject that pissed him off, but in this case, there might actually be some benefit to what he was doing. This was a good kid and it would be a shame to see him screw up his life by tying his moral compass to spurious issues or, even worse, by marrying someone just to be able to have sex.

After another sip of his coffee, he said, "Don't get me wrong, day-to-day rules can be useful, but if you come up against one of them and a spiritual commitment is important to you, it's worth checking whether that rule is based on some morality inherent in the will of God or on something more practical, like society looking out for itself. Rules are worth having, but they are interpretations and they introduce something other than 'God says' for you to consider when you make your own decisions."

Over the next few minutes, David's coffee found its way safely from the holder to his lips a couple of times as the countryside slipped past beyond the window, but he took no notice of either. He was captivated by the idea that he might explore something like sex without handing over his soul as the price of admission. But if church rules weren't going to call the shots on moral issues in his life, what was? Having to rely on his own values and his own judgment hadn't yet formed as a conscious alternative, but as his mind moved in that direction the feeling of uncertainty, of instability, was unmistakable, as if sand had begun to erode from under his feet in a fast-flowing stream.

Marvin interrupted his reflections with a change of subject.

"It's interesting, you know: When we have this kind of conversation, a lot of what I hear sounds like your old man, but there's not much of your mother in it. What does she have to say about all this?"

"You mean about sex? Come on, Marvin."

"What do you mean? How do you think she got to be your mother?"

"Oh, yuk! That's gross. I don't want to think about it."

"Women aren't just along for the ride, you know. They've got interests and hang-ups just like us."

"But this is my mother we're talking about."

Marvin looked at David and winked.

"I happen to know that your mother was part of the scene when she was younger."

"You've got to be kidding! There's no way."

"No, I'm not kidding. She was a blast. Bright and a lot of fun. She could sit in the front row in math class Monday morning and be first on the dance floor Friday night."

"Then what happened to her?"

"She met your father." After a moment he added, "That was a shitty thing to say, even if he is my brother. There's more to it than that."

"What are you talking about?"

Marvin drove in silence for a time and then made a halfhearted attempt to change the subject.

"This kind of stuff would be better coming from her."

Marvin realized he may have crossed a line. If Ruth wanted her kids to know the story, she would have told them herself. Maybe she thought talking about it would be disloyal to James. Maybe it was just too much to re-open old wounds. Who knows? Maybe, after all these years she was having second thoughts. But, goddammit, the kid had a right to know why she always copped out on morality discussions with, "Your father says ..." And he had a right to know why hugging or being affectionate wasn't her thing.

It's all a bit on the heavy side," he said eventually. "And you have to remember that it would hurt her if she found out that you knew anything before she had decided to tell you herself."

"Now you've got me worried. I will say, though, that I'm pretty good at keeping things to myself."

Marvin gave his attention to the on-coming traffic as they slowed to turn north at Massie's Corner. When they did get across the on-coming lane and start toward Flint Hill, it suited him to concentrate for a time on working up through the gears and keeping an eye on the side mirrors.

Finally, he began, "Your father wasn't the first guy in your mother's life."

As if to block the implication of what he had just heard, David said, "Of course not. She had a brother, and there were a couple of guys on her debating team. She's told me about them."

Marvin looked at him with a mix of amusement and sarcasm. "His name was Ashley Hamilton."

David felt helpless. The name meant nothing, and to respond to the implication – even to deny it – would be to acknowledge a preposterous idea. Partners were part of God's plan and the idea of his mother having another love interest was nothing short of a violation of that plan. It was wrong any way you looked at it, not to mention weird.

"Ashley's family was sort of muckety-muck," Marvin contin-
ued, "a big name down toward Leesburg, but he was an alright guy.
Rode horses and drove a T-bird, but none of that went to his head.
Good looking dude, too."

David just stared out the window.

"They met when your mother and some of the other girls in her
class were doing a service project at the Upperville Horse Show. He
apparently saw her around the fairgrounds, and the story goes that
when she was staffing the lost-and-found booth he just walked up
to her and said hello. That was it. By fall, they were an item. He'd
drive out from Leesburg as often as he could to see her. They talked
on the phone every day after school. She took an interest in horses
and would go to shows with him. I heard some years later that she
had actually started to ride. Apparently, she had a knack for it."

Something clicked with David.

"I saw a picture of her on a horse one time, but she never talked
about it."

"Her parents thought she was spending too much time with
this guy and they began to limit their time together. As spring
rolled around and the days got longer, those limits got tougher to
respect. Then one night, Ruth got home long after her curfew and
her parents met her at the door. Ashley was in the habit of waiting
in the yard until she was safely inside, so he had a front-row seat as
the shit hit the fan. They weren't going to stand by and watch her
ruin her life. She wasn't going to let them keep her away from the
person she loved.

The way I heard it, after several high-pitched versions of the
same messages, she turned and stormed back to the car. Her father
slammed the front door and turned the porch light off.

There was no way she was going to go back into that house, so
she asked Ashley to take her to her aunt's. It was late enough that
he probably should have been heading home himself, but they set

off for the aunt's place in Happy Valley. Have you ever been out that road, you know, east of Front Royal?"

"Yeah, a couple of times."

"Then you know that the Norfolk and Western rail line runs through there. There are probably a half dozen dirt roads that cross that line."

"I don't like where this is going."

"The aunt lived a mile or so off the main road. When Ashley was sure Ruth could stay with her, he left and headed home. There's a lot of guesswork in what happened next. He was probably in a hurry. He was probably tired. But we know there was no signal at the crossing and no barrier and he just drove straight into the darkened side of the train as it sped through the night.

"The train never stopped. It wasn't until a routine inspection the next morning at the Avtex plant in Front Royal that they noticed bits of the car wedged into the undercarriage of one of the tankers. It was only a matter of time then 'til they found wreckage strewn for half a mile along the tracks west of the crossing in Happy Valley. They managed to find enough of Ashley to put in a coffin."

In the silence that followed, David's mind went from the horror of what he had just heard to the realization of why Marvin had told him the story.

"Oh, my word!" he said. "She blamed herself for his death. The poor woman!"

"Yeah. To her, the whole thing was her fault. If she hadn't fought with her parents Ashley would have gone straight home."

"What on earth did she do?"

"She came unstuck. Had a real breakdown and withdrew from everybody. Flunked her year. Spent most of the time in her room and when she did go out, she didn't seem to notice people. When someone asked how she was doing she'd just stare at them.

"Then one Friday evening she wandered into the back of a church during a prayer meeting. I guess there was something about the music or the atmosphere that touched her, 'cause she went back a couple of times. That's where she met your father, and that's where she got religion. She was so grateful for the idea that God could forgive her that she skipped right over the fact that it wasn't her fault in the first place.

"To this day she lives in a space where that forgiveness gives her peace of mind. She doesn't dare do or say anything that would challenge that cocoon, and James is her guide."

"And Mummy and Daddy lived happily ever after," David said, shaking his head. "I don't know what to say, Marvin."

"What you have to say is absolutely nothing," Marvin replied emphatically. "Remember that. But maybe this will give you a better feel for why your mother behaves the way she does sometimes. If it can help you see her more as a person with her own story and less as Mother, the Flawed Superhero, then I'll be OK with having told you.

"I appreciate that. Thank you."

CHAPTER 6

By Friday following the meeting with Mr. Hanby, Jerry still hadn't returned to his usual self with the other guys, so they weren't surprised when he declined their suggestion to get together for a beer after school.

"Heavy load at the shop this weekend," he said. "I'm gonna make an early start."

In fact, when he got home, he found that there was only a light schedule for Saturday morning—a couple of winterizing jobs—so he was able to get the day off without too much flak from his father. He ducked into the house to grab a handful of biscuits for his jacket pocket and tell his mother he'd be gone tonight. It was a familiar routine and Faith Fletcher just shrugged and smiled.

"They're calling for showers in the northern Valley tonight" she called after him as he started toward the back door.

"Thanks, Mom. I'll probably head south."

She had seen the distant expression on his face when he came home so she didn't expect his usual pat or hug as he headed for the garage.

"Be careful," she called out him. She wanted to ask when he would be back, but she knew better. Fixing a time was bad for both of them. She fretted for nothing if he wasn't on time and he'd resent having to watch the clock while he was in the bush.

Gerald also assumed that his son was headed to the mountains again. He was pleased that they had become such an important part of his life, but he suspected that Jerry hunted when he was there and he worried that the more time he spent in the mountains the greater the risk that he would develop telltale patterns to his movements. Sooner or later the game warden would trip him up. But he could tell something was gnawing at his son so tonight was not the time to say anything.

Jerry pulled his camping gear from a shelf in the garage and, almost as an afterthought, reached for an extra groundsheet and a quilted vest. After all, it was almost November and there had been frost at the higher altitudes.

In fact, he had no intention of going to the mountains; he was just taking the gear so it would look like a routine trip and his parents wouldn't ask any questions. The last thing he wanted was to talk to them about what was bothering him. Did he even know himself?

"Fucking mountains," he scowled as he backed out of the driveway. Somehow the mountains were to blame for his situation. "Them and the goddamned family," he growled under his breath as he pulled out of the yard. He didn't have any plans but, from force of habit, turned west when he reached Route 211. Thirty minutes later, he had climbed over the Blue Ridge at Thornton Gap and was descending into the Shenandoah Valley.

With his usual haunts behind him, Jerry began to relax. He turned south at Luray to make his way along the South Fork of the Shenandoah River as it wandered through the gently rolling bottom land. The mountains ran along his left side now, their upper reaches still lit by the last of the sunlight. He ignored them as much as he could, scarcely looking in that direction, but at one point the road swung back to the east and through the windshield they loomed over the valley like a standing wave. He mumbled some expletive and continued to indulge in unintelligible grumbling until the road turned again to resume its southwesterly course.

Outside the village of Stanley, he slowed as the road ran alongside Hawksbill Creek. Even though he wasn't going to hunt or fish this trip, checking the water level in any stream running out of the mountains had become a habit. Fall rains usually kept these streams above their summer levels, but the rains had been sparse this year and the water was low.

Late season scavenging will be poor at higher elevations, he thought. *Bears will be on the move. There's going to be more trouble than usual for farmers with standing corn or corncribs.*

South of town the road crossed Stony Run, another tributary of the South Fork. This time he kept his foot on the brake as he crossed the little bridge and pulled the car to a stop on the shoulder of the embankment. Getting out to stretch, he walked back onto the bridge and leaned on the railing. There was still enough light for him to detect a muskrat swimming upstream near the bank, the dark spot that was the top of its head moving steadily through the reflecting surface, creating a gently waving V as it went. He flicked a pebble into the water and the muskrat submerged instantly, but a few seconds later it reappeared along the opposite bank and resumed its travel.

* * * * *

"Hi, Karen, it's Jerry."

He had stopped at a payphone in the next village and called her with no idea what he would say.

"How're you doing?"

"Well, well, if it isn't Mr. Fletcher."

It was easy for Karen Guersten to play it cool. It had been a couple of months since she last heard from him and, while she didn't necessarily think that any guy she slept with would turn out to be the man of her dreams, she had thought that the two of them hit it off at least well enough for some follow up.

"Yeah, I know," he said. "And I meant to call you, but I got busy."

"Of course, you did."

"And then, well, when too much time had gone by, I couldn't think of what to say." He waited, but Karen didn't reply. "Yeah, I guess you're right," he admitted. "Maybe this wasn't such a good idea."

There was something in his voice, or maybe it was something missing in his voice. He wasn't his usual cocky self and she decided not to end the conversation.

"I don't know, Jerry," she replied, "It's been a while, you know?"

"Yeah, you're right. And I have no excuse. But I was in the neighborhood. I was hoping you might like to go to the Chalet for a drink or something. It would be good to see you."

She hesitated, and then said,

"Just like that, huh? And how do you know I don't already have a hot date for tonight?"

Jerry smiled for the first time that week.

"Oh, maybe a little bird told me?"

"You prick, don't talk to me."

"Hell, a minute ago you were on me for not talking to you. Which is it?"

"Don't press your luck, mister. I can have the dishes done and be ready about seven."

"About seven. Yeah, that's good. I'll see you then."

Karen's cousin was one of the mechanics at the Fletchers' garage and he had introduced her to Jerry the previous summer. They had seen each other several times and her assessment was right; they had hit it off well. When they did make love, on their third date, it wasn't offhanded at all but the natural conclusion to a day and evening of closeness as they hiked and picnicked at Lewis Spring Falls on the west side of the Park. It was just that there was no place in Jerry's life for a serious relationship—except for the mountains, that is. He'd been at a loss as to how to follow up with her.

So, what was he doing calling her tonight? He would never have admitted that he needed to talk, but he wanted to be near someone. He remembered the comfort lying there in her arms and it was that comfort that drew him back. He didn't care if they slept together but he sure could use the company. He sat behind the wheel for a moment and smiled as he remembered her touch, her fragrance, the faint whisper of her breathing.

Karen was a year older than Jerry. Since her graduation she had lived with her brother and his wife on their poultry farm in Page County. She helped take care of the children and she worked in the egg room but, lately, she had also begun to show a real knack for the business end of the farm. At five hundred eggs a day, things could go wrong in a hurry, but Ed and Joan knew that they could go away for a weekend or a holiday now and, with Karen there, everything would be right when they got home.

At work and around the house she wore her blond hair up in a bun but at a picnic or on the dance floor it fell in soft waves over her shoulders. The attractiveness of her face lay mainly in its expression—familiar and inviting. Her features were too strong for cover-girl taste, but her hazel eyes could seize a passing glance and own it until she was finished with it. And her German heritage also showed in a solid build. She wasn't an ounce overweight now, but the child-bearing hips that were such killers in a pair of tight-fitting jeans were capable of someday supporting the ballast of a substantial hausfrau.

Karen had lots of first dates, and the occasional third date, but there weren't many young men willing to risk their masculinity with someone so bright and strong-willed. That didn't worry her because she had found that she enjoyed the poultry business, and her free time was now mainly taken up with an accounting course at Madison College in Harrisonburg. The challenge of the course was good in itself, but the campus bulletin boards and the conversations she overheard each week were tantalizing hints of a great big world out there. A man might figure in her life at some point, but she was in no hurry to find him.

A side entrance led directly to Karen's room, but Jerry climbed the stairs to the front porch and knocked at the main door just after seven.

"Hi," he said, somewhat anxiously, as she opened the door and stood looking at him. She wore a red sweater and black denims, and, to his relief, she smiled warmly.

"So, it's really you. And on time. I'm impressed." Without taking her eyes off him she reached down and scooped up three-year-old Thomas as he darted past her toward the open door.

"Come on in," she called over her shoulder as she carried the youngster back into the kitchen and handed him to his mother. The woodstove had been started with the first cold snap sometime in the last couple of weeks and its warmth enveloped the room.

There was a brief round of greetings as Jerry got reacquainted with the family. Then Karen pulled a leather jacket from the hall closet and they moved down the hallway toward the door, fending off kids who weren't ready to let them go. Thomas made another break for freedom, mainly for the attention, and he let out a squeal of excitement as Karen caught him easily and in one swinging motion turned him around and scooted him away from the closing door.

Jerry wasn't usually comfortable around kids and that wasn't the scene he had in mind tonight but somehow Karen's relaxed manner with the family put him at ease. By the time the door closed behind them he no longer felt the distance from her that had made him apprehensive climbing the porch steps just minutes earlier.

"So, what's the plan?" Karen asked as they reached the car. She paused and waited a moment, remembered how he always opened the door for her.

"No big plan," he answered. "I thought maybe a beer and some music. How about the Chalet?"

As he reached for the door handle, he put his left hand on the back of her arm and kept it there as she moved forward to slide into the front seat.

"Well, the Chalet will give us a beer and some music, all right," she said as they pulled out of the yard. "But it's a bit noisy on a Friday night. Are you up for that?" Realizing that the question might be too close to *What's wrong, Jerry?* she quickly added, "I've had a rough week so I wouldn't mind something a little quieter."

"Quieter is good, yeah. What do you suggest?"

"Do you like rhythm and blues?" she asked, turning sideways in the seat to face him.

"You mean like BB King?"

"Well, sort of."

"Yeah, sure."

"There's a place called the Green Door that just opened a month or so ago near the college in Harrisonburg. Do you want to check it out?"

"Are they strict about IDs?"

"You mean are they going to pull the laminate off and check the watermark? Not likely. Besides, you're with an older woman—a perfect cover."

They both chuckled and the dashboard lights reflected a sparkle in Jerry's eyes as he glanced at Karen. He was with a woman instead of the guys; he was going to hear the blues instead of rock or country; he was heading to Harrisonburg instead of some crossroads in the shadow of the mountains. He pushed himself back from the steering wheel with both hands and stretched, letting his head drop back for a moment as he exhaled audibly and smiled.

There was no way Karen was going to let herself have any illusions about this relationship, but she was pleased to see him relax. She wanted the next few hours to be good for both of them and it looked like they were off to a good start.

They had no trouble finding the Green Door. They were early for the first set, but it meant that they had their choice of seating and Karen asked for a table a bit back from the music.

"Two Buds in the bottle" Jerry said to the waiter as they settled in. "The same as last time," he added, winking at Karen.

"Actually, Jerry, I think I'll have some wine tonight. A rosé," she added, turning to the waiter.

"Mateus?" he asked.

"That'll be great, thanks." She turned back to Jerry, her smile preempting any awkwardness at the change in order, and neither of them noticed the waiter leaving to get the drinks.

The owners had done their best with a limited decorating budget. The walls and ceiling had been painted black, and draperies and reprints used to create colorful highlights around the room. Recessed lighting and wall sconces gave warmth to the setting. The tables, with their simple cloth covers set on the bias and small hurricane lamps as centerpieces, were all arranged to give a good view of a small stage at the center of one wall. Its modest array of lighting and electronic equipment, together with an upright piano, a base and several woodwind cases made it clear that this was a space devoted to music. In front of the stage was a small dance floor.

The candle at their table had settled down nicely and it contributed soft highlights to Karen's face as she leaned toward Jerry and smiled.

"I like it," she said, raising her eyebrows approvingly.

"Yeah, it's all right," he responded. "I hope the music is good, too."

The drinks arrived, and Jerry poured his beer gently into the accompanying glass. Then he raised the glass and smiled at Karen.

"I'm glad you decided to go out with me instead of that hot date."

"Yeah, well, you know, a girl's got to pace herself."

"OK. Here's to pacing ourselves." They touched glasses and, smiling, took the first sip of their drinks.

The arrival of the musicians, wearing street clothes and carrying various additional instruments, provided a diversion for their intermittent conversation. Jerry was content, only faintly aware of the disturbance that had preoccupied him all week. It hung now in the background like the shadow after a headache, reminding him of things unresolved.

"Have you ever been to New Orleans?" he asked.

"Yes, a couple of years ago. Why?"

"Oh, I don't know. Did you like it?"

"Sure, what's not to like?"

The band began its first set with a rousing number more reminiscent of Scott Joplin than the blues. These guys were good, certainly very good to the untrained ear, and they had the audience with them from the start. With each piece they moved back and forth through the world of emotions as life played itself out in day-to-day events: Love hoped for; love lost; dreams built and dreams destroyed, but always hope. The richness of the music was the richness of life, even to two young people who were just beginning to write their own lyrics. Jerry was surprised at his enjoyment of the new sound. Why should anything he wasn't familiar with have such a strong appeal to him?

They both sat silently for some time after the first set and then Karen said, "By the way, New Orleans is mainly jazz, not the blues."

"But what's the big deal?" Jerry picked up where he had left off. "I mean why go so far away just to see something in person that you can see on television in your own home?"

"You're not serious?" Karen asked incredulously.

"Sure I am. I mean to go places other people call home?"

"Oh, wow! We have got to get you out more."

"If people are happy where they live why don't they just stay there? If I have to go to Vietnam, that's different. But otherwise, I don't get it."

His reference to Vietnam distracted Karen. Two of her brothers had been drafted. One was already in country and the other had just completed his basic training at Fort Benning. He was selected for Warrant Officer training, headed to flight school.

Bringing herself back to the moment, she remembered that it wasn't beyond Jerry to pick an argument just for his amusement by saying something he didn't necessarily believe, but looking at him now, she guessed that that wasn't what was going on.

"It's just so interesting to see how other people live, Jerry, to experience it first-hand. I mean, you can't smell Cajun food on TV, or feel the night rain on your face under a streetlamp on Bourbon Street. Of course home is best, but it will always be there."

"That's just it. It may not always be there. What if you go away and things get buggered up while you're gone? How would that make you feel? I'd think that I should have been there to protect it."

Karen's eyes widened and she drew a deep breath as she sat back in her chair.

"That's heavy. Do you think about that a lot?"

"My people lost their home at the stroke of a pen. Four generations of sweat. Gone."

"That was criminal, but it was also thirty years ago. Look what your family has accomplished since. I doubt anyone is going to try to take that away."

He felt the growing frustration as he failed to convey what was troubling him. *What's the use?* He should have known she wouldn't get it. He took the last of his drink in a gulp and looked around the room, but Karen reached across the table and put her hand on his.

"I'm sorry, Jerry. Don't be upset with me. My family has never had to deal with anything like that so I have no idea what it's like."

After a moment he turned to her again,

"You know the real problem?" he said. "I don't know what I'm supposed to do about it. It's like somebody handed me this thing to take care of but nobody told me how. And then somebody else says it doesn't need taking care of, and somebody else says I need to forget it or it will kill me. Somebody else says, 'What thing?' and I have to admit I don't even know that. Is it the mountains? Is it the resettlement plot? Is it the goddamned car business?"

Both Jerry's hands were on the table now, clenched into tight fists.

Karen's fingers worked their way gently into his hair and then she slid her hand down to rest it against his cheek. He reached up with his own hand and pressed hers firmly against him, looking up to meet her eyes.

"I feel stupid talking like this, but it's just that I can't sort it out."

"Shhh," she whispered. "I wish you didn't have the problem but, if you don't mind, I'll take it as a compliment that you're talking to me about something that's this important to you."

The band had started to return for the second set. Their movements and a flurry of waiter activity before the lights went down brought the two young people back into the setting. Jerry was visibly recomposing himself but Karen didn't want the moment to be lost.

"You know, Jerry," she said, "All those things you were talking about aren't choices. They're parts of you. But there are other parts. There is only one you, and you can add new chapters to the Fletcher story if you let yourself do it." She had to emphasize the last words because the band had begun to play.

He smiled and, standing, reached for her hand.

"Let's dance."

CHAPTER 7

Oak Hill wasn't much more than the junction of two dirt roads in a remote part of the county, but its small Baptist church had an active congregation. David had spoken there on several occasions and this evening he had been invited to lead devotions during the Friday prayer service.

When it came time to head home, he had a choice: either drive ten miles out of the way to stay on main roads or take the back road, through Whorton Hollow. He decided on the more direct route.

Time alone in the car after a speaking engagement was always a time of reflection— not usually the contemplative kind, but the I-hope-I-didn't-screw-up kind. He had the empathy of a good speaker— people responded well to being cared about—and that meant he could also spot attentiveness or boredom in his audience, endorsement or disagreement.

The signals he picked up were usually positive but later, as he drove, he would sift through his presentation, reviewing responses glance by glance, looking for things he could have done better. In the end he would have to settle for his version of the qualified approval that had been the hallmark of his childhood.

But tonight's experience at Oak Hill left him uneasy on a very different score. After his brief message, he had sat for half an hour with his head bowed as different members of the congregation took turns leading the group in prayer. Most of what he heard was familiar: Gratitude for blessings received, petitions for loved ones with various challenges in their lives, and the request that God guide those in positions of power. Everyone knew the list of issues on which that guidance was needed. Everyone knew the positions God-fearing leaders had to take on those issues if the country was to avoid the evil that lurked in the plans of the ungodly. More than once the person praying would remind God of the importance of the request by saying, in a fervent tone, "Lord, we live in perilous times."

It didn't matter that they had different names or that they were praying in a different church; these were the people David knew. He had grown up among them. There were a few outliers in his life, like Uncle Marvin, but otherwise, his world was populated by versions of these same people. The same likes and dislikes, the same values. They were the chosen people. Laws, customs and mission fields had evolved to create a moral high ground for them that they took for granted. The life, the privileges they knew were a God-given right, both the promise and the charge of scripture.

But there had also been different voices tonight. A woman whose husband had recently retired to the county from somewhere in Northern Virginia asked God to watch over those who continued the struggle for equality following the passage of the Civil Rights bill. Another, a quiet voice from the rear of the room, had spoken haltingly and asked God to care for Cesar Chavez and those who worked with him in the fight against the unfair conditions of farm workers.

The room had been unusually silent during those prayers. There were none of the typical 'amen's of endorsement. But why?

And why, in that silence, was there a sense of unease? These people had prayed about things that were just as much in line with the teachings of scripture as the more familiar invocations. They had been every bit as sincere as the other worshipers, perhaps even more thoughtful. The only thing he could think of was that they had held up different people, different causes, for the Lord to bless.

David was left with a disturbing realization. That difference was the problem. The notion of *Them* and *Us* had achieved a moral standing based on nothing more than protecting what was familiar. And because belief to that effect was so widely shared, it could be accepted as truth without ever having to endure the awkward test of becoming a conscious thought. What it meant in practice was *If you want to be part of our world, be like us. Until then, if God tells us to love you, he means as a mission field, not as a member of the family.*

David had grown up in this system, but he had not realized, until tonight, how it had shaped his own attitude toward the world around him.

It may have been his preoccupation with what the evening had begun to show him, or it may just have been the rough condition of the dirt road but, for whatever reason, he didn't notice that the car had stuttered and briefly lost power a couple of times as he came down the Whorton Hollow Road.

At the bottom of the hollow, the road turned sharply to the left to follow along the bank of the Thornton River. He managed the turn easily, but when he pushed on the gas to resume normal speed there was a brief rattle from the engine and it died.

He glanced quickly at the dashboard with its red lights and then at the road ahead. The car was slowing rapidly, but in the headlights, he saw a brief widening of the right shoulder. It gave just enough room for him to pull out of the path of any traffic that might happen by. Careful not to crowd the grass strip that separated him from the steep riverbank, he turned into the space and tapped the breaks.

"That was lucky," he said aloud, despite himself.

When he turned the key, the motor turned over but nothing happened. Not even a sputter. He turned the key off again and the darkness closed in, along with the realization that he had a problem. Even in broad daylight he wouldn't have known what the issue might be under the hood. He was five or six miles from town, he had no idea where he might find a phone, and he didn't know anyone who lived in this part of the county.

This would probably add up to spending the night in the car and flagging down a passing vehicle tomorrow morning. Fortunately, with his regular trips to the mountains, he was in the habit of keeping a blanket in the car, so he'd be fine. There was no way to let his parents know what had happened but hopefully they'd assume that he could handle most eventualities.

He may have dozed off but, sometime after he had resigned himself to spending the night in the car, he became aware of headlights approaching from up ahead. Tossing the blanket to one side he stepped out to stand beside his car as the vehicle approached. The old pickup slowed to a stop as it came alongside, and the driver turned on the cab lights.

There was only one way to account for the sudden rush of adrenaline that put David on full alert. The polite term would have been apprehension; the truth was fear. He was alone, in the middle of nowhere, and the driver was a large middle-aged Negro.

It was all well and good to be in Sunday school and sing about red and yellow, black and white all being precious in God's sight; it was something else to be alone and come face to face with someone, in the middle of the night, who personified the tales of ill-will among those who weren't *Us*.

He recognized the face as someone he'd seen in town from time to time, but he couldn't find a name.

"Evenin'. Everything alright?"

The first branch of reason David grabbed was civility. Collecting himself, he answered, "No, I guess not. My car just up and died." To fill the ensuing silence, he added, "It turns over, but it won't start. It happened all of a sudden."

There was no rational way to explain David's reaction to this man. There was nothing threatening in his voice, nothing in his manner to account for the fear that gripped him as Thomas Freeman leaned over and reached into his glove compartment.

He pulled out a flashlight and said, "Let's take a look." When he opened the truck door and stepped out, he stood taller than David, and it was obvious even in the darkness that this was a man who worked for a living. A little summer employment with the Park Service and a few football practices would be no match for his strength.

"OK if I pop the hood?"

"Sure. Of course. Thanks."

It wasn't as if Negroes were a rarity in the County; everyone knew someone who hired them either as regulars or dayworkers. Some farmed and did business at the co-op, and there were a couple of tradesmen who did a steady business. But beyond the clearly defined limits of employment and service, they were not part of the mainstream community. Desegregation had stalled somewhere between law and practice, and the closest most people came to meeting them on a regular basis was to pass them going the other way in a vehicle.

For people who weren't inclined to demonize what they didn't know, this kind of separation just fed a sense of apprehension or awkwardness, a social equivalent to driving in traffic without being sure others were following the same rules. But among those always looking for someone or something else to account for their troubles, the response wasn't as benign so there were plenty of good reasons why Negroes kept to themselves.

As he watched Freeman begin a methodical check of hoses, belts, and connections, David's tension eased and his mind started to function again. It took only seconds to pick up where it had left off on what he had seen in the prayer meeting that evening: Us versus Them. But now the cloak of community was gone; the Us was him.

"I'll be damned," he murmured involuntarily.

"How's that?" Freeman asked.

"Nothing. Sorry." How could he have been so oblivious?

"Turn it over for me, will you?"

"I'm sorry, what?"

Freeman looked at him apprehensively. "Turn the motor over, please."

He got in and turned the key, but as quickly at the engine began to turn over, Freeman called out, "Stop. Stop."

David rejoined him at the front of the car and Freeman, wiping his hands on a shop rag, said, "It's your timing chain."

"And is that bad?"

"Depends. If you want to leave it here for people who are fishing to get out of the rain, no, otherwise, yes."

"That bad, huh?"

"Well, actually, if this car has as many miles on it as its age suggests, that timing chain didn't owe you anything."

"It still leaves me with the question of getting the car and myself to where we should be."

"Heading back to Washington, are you?"

"That's right. How'd you know?"

"Oh, I've seen this car a few times by the manse on Mount Salem Avenue."

David's awkwardness now had a more familiar feel.

"I'm sorry," he said. "You seem to know more about me than I do about you. I'm David Williams."

"Thomas Freeman." The big strong hand took his and shook it with practiced care.

There was an eruption of annoyed grunts from the back of the truck, confirming the smell that had settled over the area when the truck arrived, and Freeman said,

"I'd offer to run you back, but I don't think these hogs are good for many more miles before they try to break out of those crates. They have a date with the rendering pot tomorrow and I don't fancy having to chase them home on foot."

"No. No, of course not. I'll just curl up here and catch a lift with someone going in that direction in the morning."

"I've got a better idea," Freeman said. "Can you lock your car?"

"Sure."

"Good." Then, reaching between the seats of the truck, he pulled out a clean shop rag. "Pinch this in the window, then lock up and jump in the truck. I just live a half a mile back of the bridge there." He pointed over his shoulder. "We've got a phone and you can give your folks a call."

The headlights of the old truck didn't reveal much as they turned up a road just before the bridge over the Thornton River. It was more of a track than a road— rutted, with brush overhanging both sides. For the most part, they traveled in silence, but at one point Freeman said, "You know, I've got an old GMC half-ton like this one that I've been keeping for parts."

"This truck sounds like you take good care of it," David answered. In fact, he had no idea what a truck this age was supposed to sound like.

"The timing chain on that block never showed any signs of wear."

"That's good."

David had started to sense where this was might be going but didn't know how to respond. In the darkness, Freeman shook his head. White kids were clueless.

"That's the same block that's in your Chev," he explained.

"Interesting."

"New chain's expensive, but if you're not attached to a new one, maybe we could talk."

"Yes, but even if you'd be willing to part with it I'd have to convince some shop to install it for me."

"Who do you think keeps this truck up and running?"

At that point, they turned into a lane and approached a small unassuming two-story house. Even in the dim headlights, David saw that it had a fresh coat of paint. A woodpile, a machine shed, and an array of farm machinery filled the space between the house and barn; busy, but neat.

"Would you be interested in doing the repair, then?"

"Well, you know. Kind of busy these days, but I could probably work it in."

David had overheard enough conversations between his father and subcontractors to recognize the posture—The buyer always had to be hungrier than the seller. That's just the way things were done.

"If you would be interested, I'd have to check with my father. The car's actually in his name."

"Of course."

"What kind of money would we be talking?"

"Well, I'd have to have $5 for the chain. Then there's probably five or six hours in pulling it out of the pickup and installing it. A regular shop like Fletcher's would charge you about $15 an hour. And it would be better if we towed your car up here for my boy and me to work on it."

"Oh, you've got a son?"

Apparently, David knew a thing or two about negotiating after all.

"About your age, he is."

"Is his name Daniel, by any chance?"

"That's right. How do you know him?"

"I don't actually, but I saw him throwing a football one time with some other…"

His hesitation was barely noticeable. "…guys, in the field next to the practice area at school. He has some kind of arm. I wish he played for the high school team."

Freeman grunted. If he could go to the same school it might be a start, but he'd seen conversations like this go wrong too often to take a chance.

"Tell you what. How about $75 for the whole job?"

* * * * *

James agreed to drive David back to Whorton Hollow to pick up his car the following Sunday. Money changing hands on the Sabbath would have been out of the question, so David arranged to meet Thomas Saturday morning outside the house on Mount Salem Avenue to give him the cash.

When they pulled into the Freeman place Sunday afternoon Jerry recognized Daniel as the older of two boys who were tossing a football in the yard. They stopped to watch as the Suburban approached.

Jerry got out and spoke to Daniel. "Hi, I'm here to pick up my car."

"Yeah. My father's expecting you."

"Is he in the house?"

"No. He's in the back field. Oughtta be back in a few minutes."

It was strange, but the awkwardness David felt had more to do with his father's presence in this setting than with meeting Freeman's son for the first time. He turned to him and said, "It's fine, Dad. You go ahead. I'll wait until he gets back."

James looked around in a moment of indecision and then said, "OK. We'll see you later then."

"I may go by Sherry's on the way home, so tell Mom not to expect me until around supper time."

When the Suburban was gone there was some uneasy shuffling and looking about until Daniel broke the silence, "How do you like your Chevy?"

"It's good. Not going to win any trophies, but it gets me where I want to go."

"It looks all right. My father says it's in pretty good shape, too."

"Glad to hear it. I saw you tossing the ball a few weeks back, over by the high school. You've got a serious arm."

Daniel just shrugged. The youngster who had been playing catch with him when David arrived took advantage of the change of subject to try to get things going again. He clapped his hands and started to run toward the barn. Daniel threw the ball in a high arc and it settled easily into the boy's outstretched arms.

"Do you play for your school team?"

"No. I work out with them sometimes, but I've got a job after school. I don't have time to play regularly."

"That's a shame."

"There's no shame in it." Daniel said sharply.

"Of course not. Sorry. What I meant was ..." But the indignation was a cover for something else, so he left it alone. Turning toward the youngster who was walking back to them with the football, he clapped his hands together, inviting him to throw the ball. Instead, the boy looked inquiringly at Daniel.

"Go on. Throw it to him."

A spell of three-way catch ensued, with the occasional comment like "You run like a defensive end" and "Actually, that's the position I play." After about five minutes Thomas appeared on the tractor. "Afternoon, David. Sorry to keep you waiting. I see you met my boys."

"No problem, Thomas. Yeah, we were just tossing the ball."

"A tree came down across one of the fences last night. The cows would have figured it out in no time so I just had to put a few branches over the hole for the time being."

"Always something, isn't there?"

Thomas took David's keys out of his overall pocket and handed them to him. "Let's go over to the shed and see if it starts."

David shot him a concerned glance and he winked, but Daniel rolled his eyes. Catching the gesture, Thomas said, "Never mind. I can have some fun, too. Besides, you need to start getting ready to leave." Turning back to David he said, "Time to get him back to Culpeper."

It wasn't his place to ask about Culpeper, but Thomas explained. "He stays there during the week to be closer to school. From here it's a half a mile walk to catch the bus and then an hour and a half each way, what with also picking the younger kids up and dropping them off at the Scrabble School on the way."

David remembered hearing about the George Washington Carver School, south of Culpeper, the only Negro high school for Rappahannock and four other counties in the Piedmont. *Man*, he thought, *you've got to seriously want to go to school.*

Calling back over his shoulder, Thomas added, "Get a move on, now. I want to leave soon so I can get back and fix that fence before dark."

The Chev started just fine. In fact, it sounded better than before the timing chain broke.

"The carburetor was running a little rich," Thomas said. "So I adjusted it while I was under the hood. It idles better now, and you might find it uses less gas, too."

"That's great. Thank you. What do I owe you for that?"

"Nothing. Just chalk it up to me liking to have things right."

David was starting to like this man. Thoughtful, capable, an easy way with his son. And an idea occurred to him.

"Listen. I've got nothing happening this afternoon. How about I run Daniel back to Culpeper so you can get at that fencing job?"

"No, I wouldn't ask you to do that."

"You didn't. I'm offering. Let's just call it a test drive."

Thomas seemed hesitant to accept but, seeing that Daniel was still dawdling in the yard by the house, he called out. "David here says he'll drive you to town. Is that all right?"

"I don't care," Daniel replied and went to get his things together.

"There. It's settled then. Looks to me like you've got a fencing project to get to this afternoon."

"I appreciate that. Thank you."

The fact was David was glad to have the chance to visit with his new acquaintance. He pulled the car over closer to the house and then followed Thomas around as he collected tools and put them in the front-end loader of the tractor, along with a roll of fencing wire. He wasn't much help, but Thomas didn't seem to mind chatting with him as he worked.

Daniel came out of the house a few minutes later with his backpack and a shopping bag of clean laundry. A sturdy middle-aged woman appeared in the doorway behind him. She wore an apron over a dark printed dress and her hair was pulled back into a bun, looking as though she might have just taken her hat off. Still dressed from church, David recognized. The mid-day meal on Sunday was always done and settled at his house, too, before his mother got any time to herself.

As he and Thomas moved in the direction of the car, Thomas gestured toward the house, "That's my wife," he said. "Rebecca, this is David Williams."

"How do you do, ma'am. Nice to meet you." She nodded and smiled. She wasn't happy about this arrangement for her son's return to Culpeper, but she'd take that up with Thomas later.

Daniel opened the rear door of the car and put his things on the seat. Then he turned to say good-bye to his mother and his kid brother who stood beside her. But he still held the rear door open and David realized that he intended to sit in the back. As inconspicuously as possible, he cleared his throat and cocked his head toward the front seat. It worked. Daniel closed the rear door and the moment passed.

"Y'all drive careful now," his mother said.

Daniel raised his hand in a farewell gesture and held her gaze for a few moments as they started down the lane.

"Do all mothers wipe their hands on their aprons when they're saying good-bye?" David asked.

It wasn't a question that wanted an answer, but it brought Daniel's mother into the conversation. "She likes you," he said.

"Come on. We just said hello."

"You didn't call her by her first name. White folks, even strangers, usually call her Rebecca."

"It is a nice name, though."

"Right, and if I called your mother by her first name when we met, that would be cool, would it?"

"No, of course not. I didn't think of it that way."

"Is there any other way?"

Daniel had a way of setting the acquaintance clock back to zero with a single remark. David tried again.

"Are you a senior, too?"

"That's right."

"What are you thinking of doing next year?"

"I'm going to college. Already been accepted at the Hampton Institute.

"Great. I guess that's down in the Tidewater somewhere is it?

"You're pretty sharp for a white boy."

"Look. Would you rather I just drove?"

There was no answer as they turned right at the end of the lane and headed along the river to Whorton Hollow. Eventually, in what passed for a conciliatory gesture, Daniel asked, "What about you? You going to college?"

"I haven't decided. Folks expect me to go into the ministry."

"That your thing?"

"Well, I assumed it was, but I'm not so sure these days."

"Huh. Anybody ducks my head under the water, I hope he's there 'cause he wants to be."

David laughed. "And what made you decide to go to college?"

"It wasn't really a decision, it just seemed like the thing to do, if I could."

Something didn't make sense to David, but he didn't know how to raise it. Not many Negroes went on to college, so how could it be the thing to do'? But Daniel already thought he was clueless, so he just asked.

"The Talented Tenth," was the reply, as if it was obvious.

"What's that?"

Daniel rolled his eyes in silence.

"You probably never heard of a Black by the name of DuBois, did you?

"No."

"But I bet you've heard of Booker T. Washington."

"Started the Tuskegee school, right?"

"And there's nothing wrong with that. It's just that producing good workers isn't all that education is about and that's how

Washington saw it in those days. DuBois and some others pushed for Blacks to produce their own teachers, their own lawyers, their own leaders to help them ..." He was going to say escape oppression but that would have been too heavy for this white guy, so he said, "...help them find a different future. DuBois wrote about everybody getting behind those who had what it took to go to college, the ones he called the Talented Ten Percent, and that's how it became a sort of community thing."

"Isn't that a bit heavy, then—all the expectations?"

"Oh, there are a few aunts that rub it in, all right, but it kind of becomes normal. It's like if you can actually throw the ball, then it's OK for people to expect you to."

That made sense, but something else Daniel said had hung David up.

"How come you say Black? It sounds coarse compared to Negro."

"But when you say 'Negro' you're not thinking about skin color, are you? You're thinking of a class of people. That's the problem."

The truth was he'd never thought about it until this moment, but once again the prayer meeting at Oak Hill came to mind. Daniel was right: Negro was another word for Them.

"Black tells it like it is," Daniel continued. "Stokely Carmichael and the people in SNIK, man. They've got it figured out."

"SNIK?"

"Student Nonviolent Coordination Committee."

Now that David's ignorance on racial issues was exposed there was no need for hostility, and the rest of the trip to Culpeper was a first-hand primer from the other side of the racial divide.

As they passed the Fairview Cemetery and started down the hill toward town, David said, "I guess it would help if I knew where I was taking you."

"To the Lord Culpeper Hotel on Main Street."

"Oh, fancy."

"Right. If you could see my room, you wouldn't think so. Thirty hours a week for a bunk, two meals, and two bucks a day."

"Long week."

"I've got to be careful not to fall asleep in class, but I can catch a few zees on the bus." As they approached the hotel along Main Street, he said, "I appreciate the lift."

"It's no big deal," David said. "I enjoyed our conversation. Maybe I'm not quite as clueless now as I was."

"Just turn down Scanlon Street," Daniel said. "I go in the back."

CHAPTER 8

Jerry came into his father's office from the work bays late on a Thursday afternoon. "Mind if I use that green Dodge on the lot this weekend?" he asked.

"What's the matter? You tired of the Fairlane?" Gerald was in the middle of some paperwork and didn't bother looking up, so his question apparently wasn't too serious.

"No, it's just that I've got the trunk and the rear seat pulled apart. I'm trying to make things better for my camping gear."

There was enough in that excuse to take care of the inquiry, but the real reason for wanting a change of wheels was something else. Jerry was going to a different part of the Park this weekend, and he didn't want anyone connecting him with the vehicle that he'd be leaving in the parking area along Skyline Drive. Rangers, or anyone else used to seeing the Fairlane at the Meadow Springs trailhead might wonder what it was doing up at the Bluff Trail.

The other thing he needed to do before he left for the Park was make a phone call. The Keysers had been neighbors of the Fletchers on Resettlement Road following the eviction and Sam Keyser, who was about the same age as Gerald, had stayed on there after his father died to care for his mother. As far as most folks knew, he made ends meet with a large vegetable garden, a couple of greenhouses and the occasional handyman job. Jerry's mother still called in regularly or sent him by to get fresh vegetables. After school the next day, he called Keyser.

"Sam? Jerry Fletcher."

"How you doin', young fella?"

"Not so bad. And you?"

"Oh, you know. Could be worse. Got a few worms in the cabbage, but I hit 'em with the DDT this morning so they oughta be OK."

"Well, we'd better lay off the cabbage for a while then, I guess. But I was calling because Mom wants to know if you're going to be there tomorrow morning so one of us can come by and pick up her usual order."

Keyser recognized what Jerry was asking and gave him the answer he wanted to hear.

"Well, no, actually. I won't be here myself. I've got a little job I have to take care of tomorrow." Then he added, "But Annie'll be here. She'll see that you or your Mom get what you need." Annie Compton was the granddaughter of another family on Resettlement Road and she had been taking on more and more of the work in the garden and the greenhouses.

"OK, that's fine," Jerry said. "We'll just have to catch up next time."

"Right you are, young fella. Take care now, hear?"

* * * * *

About six o'clock that evening, Jerry turned into the parking area at the head of the Bluff Trail. It was late in the season for hikers and the forecast wasn't special for the weekend so it didn't surprise him that there was only one other car there. He parked the Dodge near it and, without dawdling, took a backpack and another canvas bag from the trunk, locked up and moved onto the trail. It got dark early this time of year and he wanted to cover at least a couple of miles down the eastern slope before making camp.

He managed to complete the section of the trail that wrapped around behind the Peak—the highest mountain in the county —with enough light remaining to set up camp. The canopy of autumn leaves had thinned so, from here, he'd have a view of the lowland when the sun came up in the morning. But what mattered was that, without having to clear the Peak, the sun would reach him sooner. Mornings were damned cold up here at this time of year and a bit of warmth would make it easier to get his day started.

About fifty feet off the path, next to a granite outcrop, he built a crude lean-to to protect himself from the dampness during the night. He cleared an area for a firepit and collected enough deadfall to keep a small fire going for a few hours and then make some coffee in the morning. With that done, he started the fire, used his knife to poke a couple holes in the top of a can of Dinty Moore stew and placed it next to the flames.

Good to be back, he thought, as he lay back on his sleeping bag. *And it looks like I've got the place to myself.*

The Bluff Trail was an out-and-back set up and he hadn't encountered anyone, so apparently the occupants of the other car had taken the Browntown Trail on the other side of the Drive. "Good," he mumbled, in what could have been a proprietary tone, and patted the canvas bag that lay next to him. He thought about the small meadow where he'd seen deer on previous visits and went over the route in his mind that would let him check it out as he made his way down to meet Sam.

Intermittent clouds blocked much of the sky, but he caught a glimpse of Saturn as it descended toward the Ridge behind him. Later, as he finished the stew and a half packet of soda crackers, Mars came into view above the faint haze of city lights that, seventy miles away, obscured the eastern horizon. Soon it, too, was blocked most of the time by passing clouds, but eventually it was sleep that ended his watch.

When the sun appeared, just after seven the next morning, he'd already been up for half an hour, made the fire and boiled his mix of Nescafe and sugar. Nevertheless, the hint of warmth was welcome as he proceeded to break camp.

He didn't fancy himself either a poacher or a conservationist, but Jerry had one thing in common with both: he left the smallest footprint he could when he visited the Park. When he stepped back onto the trail, the only sign that anyone had spent the night by the outcrop was a neat pile of the brush he'd used to make his lean-to. A year from now, even that would be barely detectable.

Anyone meeting him as he continued along the trail for another half-mile would have thought he was just a weekend hiker enjoying the Park. But when he reached a small creek that cut across the trail next to a gnarled oak, he stopped and looked around. Seeing or hearing no one, he stepped off the path and moved quickly, quietly, down the steep slope until he was out of sight of the trail.

It only took a minute to assemble the rifle and stow the bag in his backpack. Now, stealth became the name of the game.

It would eventually prove to be a good thing that there were no deer in the little meadow when he approached. He was disappointed, but he returned to the bank of the creek and continued down the mountain in silence, alert for any movement that might signal another opportunity.

Sam Keyser's still was cleverly hidden in the small hollow of this tributary of the Jordan River. The air that constantly slid or tumbled over the Blue Ridge and down the eastern slope dissipated any smoke from the operation, making it faint and hard to trace for anyone who might detect it downwind. There was plenty of deadfall nearby to feed the fires he needed to heat the mash. And some of the water headed for the Jordan River and eventually the Chesapeake was rerouted through pipes that Sam had rigged to cool the still.

He and Jerry had a simple honor system for moonshine trans-actions. There were always two jars of product in the corner of a toolbox in the shack. If Sam wasn't there, it was just a matter of taking the jars and leaving the money in their place. Of course, that arrangement didn't obviate the need for the telephone call. No one wanted to think about what could happen if somebody showed up unannounced when Sam was in the middle of making a batch of shine.

As Jerry descended into the hollow, he saw movement off to the right, about 200 yards away. Easily within range with the tele-scope, but the still was also nearby. If he took a shot this close it would startle Sam. Worse than that, there was always the chance that it would attract the attention of a game warden. Jerry could be long gone, no problem, but the risk was too great that the warden would then stumble onto the still. So, when he swung the rifle into position, it was just to take a look through the scope at what-ever was there.

"Son of a bitch!" he exhaled.

It was a man. What's worse, it was a man in a uniform. He was headed down the southern slope of the hollow, in the direction of the still, crouching and moving cautiously from one point of cover to another. On a hunch, Jerry swung the rifle slowly across the hollow, raising and lowering the tip to expand his field of view. On the first pass he counted four other officers. That meant there were probably more. The bastards had climbed into the Park from Bear Wallow Road, he guessed, and circled around. Now they were getting into position to raid Sam's still.

Since the law knew it was there, it was too late to save the still, but there had to be some way to help Sam. What could he do to give him time to grab anything that might be traceable and get the hell out of there? He turned to look back up the mountain in the direction he'd come, thinking through a couple of options for his climb back to the top. Then, he focused again on the shifting scene below.

The men were scattered across the valley, but he figured that, in quick succession, he could put shots close enough to at least three of them to stand their hair on end. That ought to break up the party. It would also make him a bigger prize than the still. Then he would just have to drag out the chase long enough to keep them thinking they could take him. Hell, if a grouse could lure predators away from its nest with a broken wing gag, surely, he'd be able to come up with something.

Several of the agents, including one who seemed to be giving the orders, were signaling back and forth so he figured they were about to close in on Sam. It was now or never.

His first shot exploded the radio that the leader had set on a log next to him. The second split a sapling about ear high beside another agent, and the third sent a spray of granite fragments into the pant leg of a shocked agent who had already spun to look in the direction of the shooting. All efforts at concealment for the raid were abandoned as each man dove for whatever cover he could find against the unknown assailant.

The commander shouted, "Anybody see anything?"

The third agent said, "Yeah. Muzzle flash by that hill to the right of the creek. One o'clock, 150 yards."

Apparently, fear shortened distances.

Jerry had already slipped back from the crest of the little hummock and was making his way up a ravine away from the creek. He stopped long enough to make sure the agents had abandoned their plans for the still and was relieved to hear the commander barking orders that amounted to, "Get your asses up that hill."

The big difference between Jerry and the grouse was that she showed her vulnerability by showing herself. He couldn't risk letting anyone see him, so he'd have to let his shooting be the lure. The idea would be to take a shot every few minutes to keep their attention. But, if he was too close when he fired, they might go to ground. Too far, and the commander might call them off. Either way, the point of drawing them away from Sam would be lost. So, the strategy was to find the right distance to keep their appetite up and take an erratic course to keep them from circling around him.

At one point, after several more shots, he cut back into the hollow and crossed the creek to the south side, just in time to spot two agents who had been heading up that side to get above him. The shot from a hundred yards spit tufts of moss at them from the rock they were passing; a second shot pinned them down.

Jerry checked his watch. Almost fifteen minutes had passed since his first shot. That would have been enough time for Sam to make his escape. It was also enough time for the commander to use another radio and call for support that would almost certainly include Park Police approaching along the Drive. It was time to go.

He saved a half-mile by climbing at an angle behind the Peak to rejoin the Bluff Trail closer to the parking area. As he approached the trail he found a place to hide the rifle and, minutes later, arrived at the car, winded but only slightly the worse for wear.

Shortly after he pulled onto the Drive and headed back to Thornton Gap, two Park Police cars came racing toward him, their lights flashing. As they faded in the rear-view mirror he shrugged. *Guess for now, I'll have to settle for bourbon.*

* * * * *

After school the following Friday, Jerry lifted the kitchen phone from its wall mount and gave Sam Keyser the usual call. As it rang, he jotted down the last of his mother's produce list.

"Sam? Jerry Fletcher. Yeah, it's Friday again already." He ran down the list of things Faith wanted and asked if someone would be there if he came by the next morning.

"Oh, I'll be here all right. It'll be good to see you. And by the way, ask your mom does she want some sweet potatoes. I've had some curing for a week or so and they look real nice."

When Jerry arrived at the Keyser place Saturday morning, he found Sam in one of the greenhouses. He seemed happier than usual to see Jerry.

"I've put the things your mother wanted together. They're in the cooler up front."

"Sounds good," Jerry replied, but Sam hadn't finished.

"All but the sweet potatoes, that is. Grab one of those baskets." He pointed to a stack of wooden six-quart containers, "And come on out back."

When they were well clear of the greenhouse, he stopped, glanced around, and turned to Jerry.

"I'm thinking you might have had something to do with solving a problem I had on a job last week."

Jerry looked around casually as if he was taking in the scenery, checking again that they were alone. Then he winked at Sam.

"Sometimes it just works out, I guess, that you're in the right place at the right time."

"Yeah, well you saved my ass, man. That's all I can say. I sure as hell appreciate it." Jerry just smiled, and Sam continued.

"I was able to grab my tools, and a fuel can that probably had my prints all over it and get the hell out of there. I'm sure everything else is destroyed by now. Those bastards got no respect for superior workmanship." He smiled at the hint of sarcasm he'd been able to muster, but there was no doubt he had lost his labor of love.

"I'm sorry, Sam. It'll be good if they don't figure you out, but that doesn't help with what you lost."

"Yeah, but if it wasn't for you, man, things could have been a lot worse. I figure I'd better lay low for a year or two in case they're watching me. I'll give you the name of a friend over to Luray who'll take care of you in the meantime. He makes a pretty decent product."

"I appreciate that."

"Just be sure to tell him I sent you."

Sam stopped by a waist-high mound of straw. "I haven't heard anything about anybody being shot out this way lately, so I guess them Feds were lucky you're not inclined to vengeance." He pushed the top layer of straw to one side, revealing sweet potatoes.

"What are you talking about?"

Sam started to put some of the tubers in the basket.

"Did your folks ever tell you about your Great Uncle Jeb?"

"Rings a bell. A preacher, wasn't he?"

"That's right. Back on the mountain. They weren't much as churches go; just little groups of people who met every Sunday at somebody's house in one hollow or another. But Jeb would walk from one to the other with his old King James Bible in his satchel and minister to them – I guess that's what they called it – as best he could."

"That's all very interesting, Sam, but I don't see what it's got to do with anything."

"Do you know how he died?"

"It was an accident of some sort, if I remember."

"Only if you call a full load of buckshot at close range an accident."

Jerry wondered why he hadn't heard this story, but for the moment he just stared at Sam, incredulous.

"Who'd he piss off?"

"Nobody. That's the point. He was what you'd call a victim of circumstance."

"What kind of circumstance?" Jerry didn't know whether Sam was being careful or just spicing up the story with a hint of mystery. Either way, he was getting impatient.

"Folks had it rough in those days. Poor land to farm and not much by way of skills to get what jobs there were. They didn't have money most of the time to support a preacher, so they'd give him stuff. Food, household things, and sometimes 'shine. This was in the 20s and Prohibition was on, so he had to be careful, but if Jeb managed to sell the shine to one of the runners in the county he'd have a bit of cash for him and the family. Hear tell, though, he often spent that on others he felt were worse off than him and his."

"You seem pretty up on the story of somebody who wasn't even kin," Jerry said.

"Well, your Uncle Jeb's story probably didn't get much play in your family 'cause of the 'shine part, but my grandaddy was a moonshiner – one of the best in the county— so on our side, hell, moonshine was family.

"Anyhow, one spring morning a couple of guys from one of Jeb's churches found his body in the ditch coming out of Nicholson Hollow. They knew it was revenuers who shot him, 'cause the same buckshot that killed him was used to waste the can of shine he was carrying. Nobody but a revenuer is dumb enough to waste a perfectly good gallon of whiskey."

Jerry's first thought was that something was missing; there had to be more to the story. But part of him locked onto the familiar theme: Government agents don't give a damn for people's lives.

"The revenuers normally arrested guys with shine and held them for some court or other, so nobody knows why Uncle Jeb got shot. He never carried a gun and there was no sign of a fight, so I guess one of the government guys must have been having a bad day."

Staring across the road toward the mountains, Jerry didn't say anything.

"That was thirty years ago, but I kinda got to thinking this week how the tables might have been turned up there in the Jordan hollow," Sam concluded.

"I guess you're right," Jerry said. "It's probably just as well I didn't know that story."

A few minutes later, as he headed for the car with his produce, Sam called after him, "Tell you mom those sweet potatoes would probably roast real good."

CHAPTER 9

It wasn't the morning full of Sunday school and church that made Sunday such a long day in the Williams household; it was the afternoon and evening full of nothing. Sunday, being a day of rest, there was of course no work, but there was also no play. Anything that involved exertion or that detracted from the devotional order of the day was forbidden. Even after James gave in and bought a television for the family, he forbade its use on Sunday. David had to wait until Monday morning to learn how the Washington Redskins had fared, or his back-up football team, the Baltimore Colts. After all, who could not love a team with Johnny Unitas as its quarterback?

Reading or listening to music, going for a walk, visiting like-minded friends—the practical rule was that anything you could do in your church clothes without messing them up was OK, except watching TV, and, of course, woe to anybody caught doing homework on Sunday.

David was acutely aware of these restrictions on a Sunday in early November. He had been asked to speak the following Sunday at the Piedmont Baptist Church over in the Francis Thornton Valley and working on that sermon would be OK, but he was also facing a biology test the next day that he wasn't ready for.

Sitting in the back yard after lunch he came up with a solution. On such a gorgeous fall day it would be good to be outside, so he'd take his books and go somewhere out of town. He'd spend time thumbing through his Bible looking for a passage and a subject for his sermon, but he would keep his biology textbook handy, too, and work in some study time. On balance, the Lord would probably be OK with that, even if his father wasn't.

Such a distinction would have been unthinkable even a year earlier and to James it still was.

On more than one occasion he had told David, "The Lord has given me a special gift. He speaks directly to me and I understand His will more clearly than others do."

In his early years, David had been awestruck by the immediacy of this connection to the Almighty and it had made him less inclined to argue with his father or ask twice for anything. But lately, he had begun to test his own convictions and found that, strangely enough, he could be at peace on some issues where his position differed from his father's. Perhaps it wasn't coincidence that, along with this discovery, David was beginning to think his father's sense of spiritual infallibility had more to do with his personality than with his connections.

James had come by the strength of his convictions honestly. His father, Will, had been a horse trader. Sometimes he even traded horses, but Will was always looking to make a deal. That was not only his obligation as a father of twelve during the Depression; it was his personality. Convinced, single-minded and driven. Admitting uncertainty or ambivalence was, at best, a poor negotiating tactic and, at worst, a sign of weakness. Even after he slowed down with age and settled in a small cottage south of Winchester, he always seemed to have an agenda or an opinion he wanted his listener to endorse. He had a point to make and he would persist until his listener acknowledged it.

One day James had returned to the car after a heated discussion with his father in the yard outside the cottage, a confrontation that David could only monitor by their exaggerated gestures as he watched through the closed car window. After a moment of deep breathing to regain his composure as he clenched the steering wheel, James said, to no one in particular, "You know the trouble with that man? If he's selling year-old hay it's as good as new-mown but if he's buying it, it's not worth straw."

The clarity with which Will saw the right way to do things made it easy for him to see the error in the ways of others and he wasn't concerned about where or to whom he expressed that judgment.

It had fallen to James' mother to make peace in Will's turbulent wake, and when James spoke of Alice it was always with a sense of awe. She was such a godly woman, he would say, so dedicated to her faith and her family. The stress of bearing and raising a dozen children during the Depression put inordinate demands on her health and Alice had died when David was eight. Prior to her death, visits to the grandparents' home had been few and far between, so he didn't have many personal impressions of her, but certainly nothing about the quiet, smiling old lady directing activities from a cot to one side of the kitchen would contradict the saintly picture his father had created.

As one of the middle children in such a large family, James had found that competing for his mother's attention in this frenetic household was not easy. But he learned early on that showing an interest in her faith—quoting a verse from scripture or asking a question from a Sunday school lesson—was the surest way to capture a few moments of one-on-one time with her. As he began to offer his own take on the spiritual truth of whatever topics they were discussing, her approval became the most important validation of his adolescence.

Provided the particular position his son took in these conversations didn't contradict something Will was espousing at the time, he took James' growing sense of conviction as proof of his own parenting skills and that had led to James spending more time with his father on various projects. So an assertive posture on things of the spirit had earned favor for James in the eyes of both parents and set him on his own path to lay preacher and authoritarian parent.

* * * * *

Fortunately, the biology text was still in the car with his other schoolbooks, so David went to his room, retrieved his Bible, and announced in a light-hearted tone that he was going to drive out Fodderstack Road and go for a walk.

There was a chorus of "I wanna go, too" and "Oh, Me too. Me too," and David turned to his mother with a silent plea. Ruth had recognized his growing need for space as he reached his later teens, and she intervened now to help him deflect the requests. In a matter of minutes after devising his plan he was in the car pulling away from the house.

He knew of a dirt road a couple of miles out of town that went up Salem Hollow toward the base of the Park. It was a private road on land owned by the Corbins, members of the church, and they had often invited David and others to use it as a jumping-off point for hikes into the Park. The Corbins lived in town now, so the chances were good that he'd have the area to himself and the setting suited him. For the last three hundred yards before it entered the hollow the road traversed a high open meadow. Looking to the southwest from that point he would have a perfect view of Old Rag and he knew the scene would be spectacular. All the other mountains would be paying homage in their fall colors to the most prominent peak on the eastern side of the Blue Ridge. He just hoped that it would inspire a sermon and a decent grade in biology.

When he reached the meadow, he pulled off the track into the long grass and dried stalks of wildflowers, turned the car toward the southwest and stopped. As promised, Old Rag dominated the horizon, muted somewhat in an autumn haze and anchored on either side by the closer peaks of Jenkins and Red Oak mountains. After wandering about the meadow for a few minutes he pulled his Bible and his biology text out of the car and climbed onto the hood. Leaning back against the windshield he let a slight breeze from the northwest put the finishing touches on a perfect setting.

Lord, when I see Your creation laid out like this, I feel close to You, he began, praying in silence, but as casually as someone might speak to a friend.

You know my needs. You know my doubts about how I can best serve You. Guide my thoughts for next week, Lord, and my studies for school.

For the next hour he browsed back and forth through his well-worn copy of the King James Bible. First, he thumbed through the New Testament: The Gospels, the Acts of the Apostles, the Letters to the Churches. He reread well-known verses and randomly started chapters from the opening verse. In the past, he had put notes in the margins next to verses that had struck him during sermons or bible studies and he reread those notes.

From time to time he would raise his eyes and let words or passages turn over in his mind as he scanned the horizon, catching the turn of a red-tailed hawk or the shadow of a patch of cloud rising against a distant slope. But nothing he reflected on triggered an idea for his sermon.

He flipped back to the Old Testament. Fewer notes, fewer well-known verses. Tricky to preach from, because it predated Christ and Baptists generally expect their preachers to build their sermons around the Gospel.

He had to admit that he found some of the things he had heard in the name of prophecy to be a bit weak—really stretched if truth be told. It never crossed his mind to question the value of God's teaching before Christ, but he couldn't help thinking that some of the lessons preachers tried to read into that teaching were far-fetched. What's more, Bible teachers weren't inclined to encourage everyday folk to read the Old Testament without the benefit of counsel; there were things like wife swapping and drinking during religious holidays that needed some explanation. The Psalms were always safe, but what could a seventeen-year-old guest preacher add to a Psalm?

This was getting him nowhere fast, so he decided to take a break and look at some biology. General Biology by Johnson, Laubengayer & DeLanney lay on the hood beside him. The size of the book alone was enough to get a guy off to a bad start. It had to weigh at least four pounds and its six hundred and fifty pages had more Greek names than the roster of enlisted men in the Trojan Wars. In less than eighteen hours he would be tested on the human body systems, one hundred and sixty-five pages on everything from the skeleton to the reproductive system.

He chuckled to himself as he recalled his father's indignant reaction on seeing the text at home one evening. Browsing through it he had happened across explicit diagrams and descriptions of the male and female anatomy and exclaimed, "What does he need to know that for? He's not going to be a doctor."

* * * * *

The following Sunday morning David set his Bible and his notes on the pulpit of the Piedmont Baptist Church and looked out over the congregation. He recognized most of the thirty or so people present, including some of his classmates.

"Thank you, Deacon. Good morning, Folks. It's a privilege to be asked to share this time of worship with you this morning," he said. "Let's begin by asking God's blessing on our time together."

He closed his eyes and began to pray. "Heavenly Father, we have come together this morning to worship You and to listen to You. Speak to us now, Lord, as we look into Your word together, for we pray it in Jesus' name, Amen."

Everyone looked attentively toward him. He knew from years of listening to other preachers and hearing his own father talk about the process of preaching that he had about two minutes to catch their attention if he wanted to keep them with him for the fifteen to twenty minutes he planned to speak. Humor often worked, or current events, or a personal anecdote.

"Before I ask you to turn with me in your Bibles to today's passage, I want to share an experience with you. When I say that it's a privilege to meet with you, it's not just true because this time of worship is precious to all of us, but because of the special challenge it presents for me. Every time I'm asked to speak I begin to plan with the same question in my mind: What could a seventeen-year-old possibly have to say to folks who have experienced so much more of life than he has?"

He left the question there for a moment, giving the adults a chance to appreciate his honesty and acknowledge their own doubts. The young people were watching now, to see how he was going to get himself out of this one.

"The only thing I can say is that, after a couple of years of visiting churches and having these opportunities, it now takes me less time than it used to to realize my mistake."

Again, a pause, but the lights came on in a number of faces, so he didn't delay.

"Right! As the Apostle Paul said, 'Not I, but Christ in me'. And I had the clearest example you could imagine of the Lord speaking to me as I was thinking last week about this morning's message."

David went on to describe his drive to Salem Hollow and his fruitless search through the scriptures for a topic for this morning. Then, he described how he had given up after a couple of hours and headed back to town, how he'd noticed a weathered old mailbox on Fodderstack Road, with fresh lettering announcing the new resident's name: Samuel Jamison.

"Samuel! Of course! Samuel, the young man promised to God by his parents. Samuel, the young man serving God in the temple among older men. Now, with my concern about being a young man in the Lord's work, wouldn't you say He was trying to tell me something?"

There was a chorus of amens across the room and a wave of approving nods.

"And the other thing about Samuel that made him relevant for me? The Lord had to call him four times before he got his attention. On any school morning my mother would have seen the connection immediately!"

There were smiles and outright laughter in the room and family members looking at each other with a wink or a nod.

"My search through scripture that afternoon had simply prepared me to receive a message from God. My antennae were out."

Again, there was a chorus of amens.

"So guess which book I turned to when I got home..."

A dozen voices said "Samuel".

"Uh Huh! And guess where we're going to turn now!"

There was a wave of approving chuckles.

"I'm confident that the Lord has a message for us as I ask you to turn with me to 1st Samuel, Chapter 3." After a few moments of silence broken only by the rustle of pages, he added, "Let's begin with verse 3."

David read the next nine verses clearly but quickly, setting out the story of Samuel being called in the night by God and how, each of the first three times, Samuel gets up, goes to Eli, the high priest, and says, "Here am I," only to be told that Eli didn't call him and how it finally occurs to Eli what's going on. He tells Samuel what to do and when God calls the fourth time Samuel responds with "Speak, Lord, for thy servant heareth."

"Now, Folks, you might be tempted to say that Samuel was a bit slow on the uptake. I mean, three wake-up calls and he's still in a fog. What's going on here? But you know, if we put ourselves in his shoes, I think we might see some of the things that get in the way of hearing the Lord when He calls us, too. Let's look at verse three again.

"'And ere the lamp of God went out in the temple of the Lord, ... Samuel was laid down to sleep.'—This kid fell asleep with the lights on."

There were chuckles throughout the room and David continued, "Now, I don't know about you, but when that happens to me it usually means I'm really tired. As the assistant to Eli in the temple you can be sure Samuel's days started early and went long. So he crashed as soon as he had finished his work and he was dead to the world. You can imagine the poor bleary-eyed kid, when he hears his name being called, picking himself up from his mat, wrapping the blanket around himself and staggering off to the other room to see what Eli wanted. After all, there were only the two of them in the temple at this hour of the night, right?

"The first time God called, Samuel was too tired to hear Him," David summarized and then with a wink continued, "But, Lord, wrestling's only on at 11:30 Saturday night. I had to stay up late. Right, gentlemen?"

There was a chuckle and some shifting in seats.

"But, Lord, I just couldn't put that novel down. I kept saying to myself, just a few more pages. Right, ladies? And often it's not even the little pleasures we allow ourselves; it's trying to squeeze that extra chore into the day. But whatever it is, we need to recognize that being tired cuts into our ability to hear God, to recognize Him when He calls.

"Eli probably thought the boy had been dreaming and he just said, 'I didn't call you. Go back to bed'. Imagine how relieved Samuel must have been to find that he could go back and curl up on his mat!

"Now verse 6: 'And the Lord called yet again, 'Samuel'. And Samuel arose and went to Eli and said, 'Here am I' and this time he adds, 'for thou didst call me.' I don't think Samuel was being rude. He probably just wanted to get on with things. I'm here. Now what is it you want me to do?

"By now Eli is beginning to wonder about this kid. We're told earlier that his work around the temple had met with the favor of both God and men, but this hearing things in the middle of the night…. Maybe there's a problem."

Quiet laughter rippled across the congregation.

"But, folks, what happens when we're working really hard and we fall asleep? I wouldn't admit to you that I ever leave studying to the last minute." He looked at several of his classmates in the congregation. "None of us would, right?" Family members sitting together exchanged muffled snorts and glances.

"But let's just say that there are times when I have to study very hard. When I finally do crash, I may zonk out but it's not very good sleep. And when I wake up, my mind just picks up where it left off, like it's on automatic. I'll bet when the alarm went off this morning some of you were halfway out of bed and headed back to your to-do lists before you remembered that today was Sunday." It was clear from their reaction that most of the congregation knew what he was talking about, and David pulled things together again.

"The first time God called Samuel he was too tired to hear Him. The second time God called he was too busy to hear Him.

"Eli and Samuel are probably both a little more awake now. Samuel is thinking that the old fella may be a bit touched. Eli is wondering about the youngster's sleep habits, and he decides to be firmer. 'I didn't call you, My Son. Go back to bed.'

"Now verse 8: Sure enough, the Lord called Samuel a third time. The poor kid's at a loss, but he dutifully gets up again and goes to Eli. You can almost hear the frustration in his voice. 'Here am I,' he says, 'because thou didst call.'

"Watch what happens next, Folks! Somebody gets a wakeup call and it's not Samuel.

"'And Eli perceived that the Lord had called the child.'"

David paused for a moment and waited for most eyes to be on him.

"Why do you suppose it took so long for Eli to put the pieces together? Maybe it's just that he was tired, sure, but could it also be that he didn't expect that God would communicate with the child? After all, he was the high priest. If God was going to speak to anybody, it would be him, right? Maybe he had been in the job for so long that he took his role for granted. Maybe he had become complacent.

"And if Eli didn't expect God to communicate with the child, where would Samuel ever have come up with the idea? We know he had been raised to worship God, and to want to serve Him, but the Lord's plans for Samuel exceeded not only his own expectations, but those of Eli and his parents, and no one had taught Samuel to be ready for such a possibility.

"How many times have we seen an opportunity to step beyond the limits of our experience, to serve the Lord in some new capacity?

And how many times have we responded 'Me, Lord? Little old me? You want me to do what?'"

David paused. The congregation assumed he was letting the thought sink in, but he had stumbled on his own words. This idea of having the confidence to act on conviction, to tackle something beyond our comfort zone, was scripturally sound. But his own instinct to play it safe had left him with the uncomfortable feeling of having told people to do as I say, not as I do.

He took a sip of water and refocused.

"So, when it finally dawns on Eli," he continued, "that God is trying to talk to Samuel, he tells the young man to go back to bed, but this time he tells him what to expect and what to say.

"I don't think the poor kid got much sleep this time, do you? Imagine lying there waiting to see if God is going to speak to you. Man, when I was his age, I had enough trouble trying to get to sleep on Christmas Eve with one ear out for reindeer on the roof!"

Smiles and laughter told David the congregation was still with him.

"Everyone in this room knows the expression Three strikes and you're out. Aren't we lucky God doesn't work that way? We'd all have been in trouble a long time ago! And look at Samuel. The poor kid blew three chances to talk with God. He was too tired. He was too busy. He was too modest. And now he's lying there bug-eyed in the middle of the night wondering if he'll get another chance. He's probably as afraid of it as he is anxious for it.

"And then what happens?

"Verse 10: 'And the Lord came, and stood, and called as at other times, Samuel, Samuel,' and Samuel answered as Eli had taught him, 'Speak, for thy servant heareth.' And the Lord went on to reveal his plans to Samuel, saying 'I will do a thing in Israel, at which both the ears of everyone that heareth it shall tingle.'"

David closed his Bible slowly, purposefully, and stepped out from behind the pulpit.

"Folks, even though the story of Samuel is the story of a remarkable young man and wonderful parents, it's also the story of a person who experienced some of the same difficulties we all do in hearing the Lord when He calls us. Sometimes we're too tired. Sometimes we're too busy. Lots of times we're too modest. And from Eli we learn that sometimes we're complacent. But if we can overcome these obstacles and be attentive to the voice of the Lord, He will speak to us. He will show us what He wants us to do."

He moved to the edge of the platform, smiling enthusiastically as he scanned the congregation.

"And just imagine the excitement, the blessing," he concluded, "when the Lord comes to you and says, 'I'm going to do something that will make their ears tingle'!

Let's pray."

CHAPTER 10

Jerry saw the fist coming through the shadows and dodged just in time. Hack Dodson lost his balance as his swing went on through and in the split-second before he could recover, Jerry struck back, pounding his assailant across the side of the head. Hair and flesh muffled the impact but there was no doubt when Dodson hit the ground that he was going to stay there for a while.

"Now, which one of you mother fuckers wants to continue this conversation?" Jerry's words were crystal clear, despite the beer that coursed through his system. He couldn't recognize all of the figures in the late evening shadows, but it didn't matter. It was the same old bunch. So why had Dodson swung at him?

"I got no beef with you, Jerry," replied Billy Atkins, who stood closest to Jerry. "Not me."

It was Saturday night and he and some of the other guys had been driving with Hack Dodson when they happened on Jerry and a couple of seniors in the vacant lot back of the general store in Sperryville.

"Me neither," Tommy Corbin chimed in. Not everyone spoke up, but no one seemed ready to fight either.

"Come on, Jerry, you know us. A good time, man, no sides." Atkins continued to try to defuse the situation.

As a rule, it didn't matter that the guys switched back and forth between Dodson and Jerry, depending on who showed up with the wheels and the beer on a given weekend and normally, when the two met, everyone would pool their resources and continue to party. But in the last couple of weeks the guys thought Jerry had been acting kind of weird. He hadn't gone out much on weekends and he kept to himself after school, so they had gravitated to Hack; it was his car that was usually full when it left the school lot or when it headed for Earl's to buy beer. Hack had begun to dig his new role as top-dog and it had only taken a six-pack for it to get him in trouble.

"What the fuck's with him, then?" Jerry asked, speaking to no one in particular as he gestured toward the figure on the ground that had begun to stir.

"Ah, never mind him, Jerry. He's pissed, that's all. Just let him sleep it off and he'll be back to his old self."

Things seemed to have cooled down and Jerry and the others started back toward the street.

"Where you been lately, Jerry? We ain't seen you much."

Atkins was curious but he was also making sure the situation had quieted down.

"Oh, I've been around. I just had some things I had to do," Jerry replied.

Then, a hoarse voice shouted after him from the yard.

"Hey, you fuckin' hillbilly. Where you think you're goin'?"

Jerry went cold. He stopped and turned slowly. In the dark shadows he could barely make out Dodson standing, his feet apart, slapping a stout stick into the palm of his hand. Two others had decided to cast their lot with him, and they stood on either side. Roddy Jenkins held a trash can lid that he tapped nervously against his thigh and Jed Connolly was wrapping something around his fist.

"What did you say?" Jerry asked, buying time to see which way things would go.

"You heard me, mountain boy. You think you and yours can just come down out o' them hills and take over anytime you please? You got another thing comin'."

Jerry had heard hints of this kind of sentiment over the years, the occasional muffled remark. Once he had overheard his father comforting his mother in the kitchen when she came home crying from Mowatt's store.

"Never mind" his father had said. "It's just talk." But those had been real tears as she clung to him and sobbed.

Now the young Fletcher took a couple of steps toward the menacing form.

"Call it back, Dodson," he said in a flat voice.

"Why don't you put a little moonshine on your tail and take it home to Momma?" Hack taunted. The snicker from Jenkins was more nerves than support, but instinctively he and Connolly positioned themselves off Dodson's shoulders as Jerry advanced toward the figure that continued to slap the stick rhythmically into his open hand.

"Dodson, you don't want to do this" Jerry said, "I'm telling you one more time, call it back."

"Faith, isn't it? Fancy name for a woman that sleeps with a hillbilly." Dodson seemed oblivious to his own peril. "She keep you warm at night too, does she, mountain boy?"

Jerry snapped. He launched himself at Dodson in the same instant as the stick rose, but he was inside the range of Dodson's swing before it started down and he drove his fist into the exposed ribs as he passed under the arm. The impact slowed his momentum enough that he could follow with a roundhouse that struck Dodson's biceps. His arm went limp and the stick spun to the ground.

Jenkins and Connolly closed on Jerry at the same time. The lid crashed harmlessly against his shoulder but the buckle of Connolly's belt tore shirt and flesh as his fist found its mark in the small of Jerry's back. He wheeled on the two and made instantly for Jenkins, grabbing his shirt, and levering himself forward to smash his forehead into Roddy's face before he could muster a defense. The scream told the story even before the blood began to gush from his nose.

Jerry released him and dropped to the ground to avoid the attack he knew was coming from Dodson. Rolling in the direction of the stick, he groped for it in the darkness and swung knee high at the remaining two attackers. He missed, but the gesture kept them at bay while he regained his feet.

Dodson's right arm hung at his side, but he had something new in his left hand.

"Come see your momma, mountain boy," he hissed, and this time he was ready as Jerry came at him again.

Without glancing sideways Jerry drove the stick hard into Connolly's stomach as he passed, knocking the wind and the fight out of him, but he arrived off-balance in Dodson's range and fell to the ground as the iron pipe struck his thigh. The pain was immediate, searing, but he continued to roll and took Dodson down. Emerging on top, he punished the injured arm with one knee as he pinned the pipe with the other and landed a fist on the side of Dodson's head.

A frightful series of blows followed as Jerry spent his fury on the form struggling beneath him. The stories around town the following week would include graphic descriptions of the sound that rattled from his throat as he struck his target, but he didn't hear it. He ignored the others shouting at him to stop and, when arms reached for him and closed around him, he fought them as if they were extensions of Dodson.

In fact, someone had called the Sheriff's office and two deputies had arrived to break up the fight. He broke one deputy's nose and cracked a couple of ribs on the other before a nightstick put an end to his rampage. He went down like a shot steer and lay motionless as they put the handcuffs on him.

The ride in the back of the cruiser and the booking at the Sheriff's office went by in a blur of pain and embarrassment. Nursing their injuries, the deputies weren't taking any chances with him. They would have preferred to put him in a cell but they were for adults.

"Goddamned red tape," Deputy Jackson muttered as he and Deputy Foster steered Jerry to a small spare office. Jenkins was a mess, with dried blood in smears and ridges over his face, neck and shirt, and rivulets of blood still wet under his watering eyes. The pain had eased enough that anger now ruled his behavior. He pushed Jerry into the room and, as Foster stood by the door with his nightstick drawn, he jerked Jerry around and removed the handcuffs.

"Now you set over there," he said, pointing to a wooden chair in the corner, "And don't you move 'til I come back for you."

Jerry had begun to seethe at himself for getting into this situation but, as the two uniformed officers left the room and swung the door closed, he had to fight a sudden sense of panic as the walls started to close in.

"Just breathe," he said to himself, "Just breathe." God, what he wouldn't give for a swig of shine. *Not even a window,* he thought as he glanced about the room, but he continued to concentrate on his breathing and gradually felt some relief.

As the panic eased, he took stock of his situation and realized something that should have been obvious earlier. He was the only one that had been booked. Maybe he had assumed the other guys were just being patched up before being brought in, but they would have been here by now. No, he was the only one being charged. What sort of a story had those bastards put together while he lay unconscious in the yard? And what sort of law would just assume that he had gone looking for trouble? Probably the same law that would chain a man to a tree and load his possessions on a truck.

By 3 AM Jerry knew the extent of the damage. He had been charged with assault and battery, two counts of assaulting a police officer, disorderly conduct, and drinking underage. The full weight of the charges didn't register on him, but they sounded pretty serious. All that for shutting Dodson's smart-ass mouth. *How was I supposed to know they were cops?*

He breathed a sigh of relief that he had parked out on the street, where his car wasn't recognized and searched. If they had turned up the mason jar he kept under the tarp in the trunk he could have lost the car and his license, and there would have been all sorts of questions about his connections in the mountains. It wasn't unusual to have a jar of local whiskey in the trunk or under the seat, but it was a sure hook for extra charges if the cops were so inclined.

Later that night, Jerry was released into his father's custody.

"What the hell were you fighting about?" Gerald asked, breaking the strained silence on the drive back to Flint Hill.

"Oh, nothing. Dodson was being an asshole, that's all."

"That's no excuse for you to go messing up your life. What the hell were you thinking?"

"I didn't think."

"You bet your sweet ass you didn't think."

"Look, Dad. I screwed up, all right? I'll take the consequences. Can we just drop it?" His head was throbbing.

Gerald didn't agree or disagree, but he didn't pursue the matter. He knew his son didn't lose his temper easily, and he had a hunch what might have set him off. All he said was, "You'd better make peace with your mother when we get home. She's pretty upset."

When they reached home, Gerald pulled into the lighted parking area between the house and the shop.

"Go into the shop and get cleaned up before she sees you," he said, gesturing toward the side door. "I'll tell her you're checking on the compressor."

As they passed each other in front of the car Gerald reached out and stopped Jerry with a hand on his shoulder. The younger Fletcher looked apprehensively into the stern face. It seemed as though his father wanted to say something but, finally, he just squeezed his shoulder and growled.

"Get out of here."

* * * * *

Two weeks later the Fletchers had their first meeting with Caldwell Perkins, the attorney they had engaged to defend Jerry. A studious, well-dressed man in his early forties, Perkins had developed a very successful practice in Fairfax County based on his rigorous defense of juveniles charged with violent crimes. He made a point of telling potential clients that he wasn't going to help them beat the law, but he would be sure it was applied fairly.

As part of his initial investigations, he liked to meet with his clients in their homes if possible, to get a sense of the environment in which his charge was raised, to see the interaction with his parents and to start the attorney-client relationship in a familiar setting. The Fletcher home didn't host too many Brooks Brothers suits but Perkins wore his so comfortably that it seemed natural enough as they all sat around the kitchen table. In the short time since arriving, he had formed the impression of a strong family whose circumstances afforded plenty of outlets for the horsepower of a solid young man like Jerry. Whatever lay back of the events behind the Sperryville corner store that night, it wasn't simple rebellion.

He explained that, since it was still three months until Jerry's eighteenth birthday, he was a juvenile in the eyes of Virginia law. Since the state did not have a separate juvenile court system, his case would normally have come under the Rappahannock County District Court, the local jurisdiction that dealt with the bulk of misdemeanors, traffic violations and juvenile and domestic relations cases.

"However," Perkins continued, "There is a provision in the law whereby charges against a minor for violent crime can be tried in a higher court. The presiding district court judge only needs to certify the charges and the case is transferred to the circuit court. Jerry's case is going to the circuit court."

At first blush, this seemed to the Fletchers like so much bureaucratic mumbo-jumbo. The two judges used the same courthouse on Gay Street and presumably they applied the law the same. Jerry was nervous enough about his whole situation that he sat silently, but Gerald asked impatiently, "So, what's the difference?"

Faith slid her chair back noisily, stood and moved toward the kitchen counter.

"More tea anyone?" she asked, fidgeting with the kettle.

"I'm fine, ma'am," Perkins answered and then looked at Gerald.

"Well, there's a big difference, actually, Mr. Fletcher. Let me give you the bad news first. District courts deal with cases that carry a sentence of twelve months or less in jail or, in the case of a minor, in a juvenile detention center. But circuit courts don't normally hand down sentences of less than one year and they are served in state prison." Jerry's gut tightened and he heard his mother gasp.

"Now just a moment," Perkins cautioned. "Sentences are only for those found guilty. We are going to contest these charges because we believe they are not supported by the facts."

His firm tone and measured pace had the desired effect. The tension eased and he had the Fletchers' undivided attention.

As a defense attorney with twenty years of experience in judicial circuits throughout Northern Virginia, Caldwell Perkins never ceased to be amazed at the naiveté of everyday citizens caught up in the web of the law. It was a good system. He still believed that. But did people think that judges took off their human nature when they put on their robes? That cops didn't have good days and bad? And with about three million cases in the State system every year, didn't people understand that there had to be a structure to deal with the load, a structure staffed with thousands of people who got no closer to the facts of a case than the paperwork and the schedule?

Perkins also worked as a volunteer with young people outside the court system, and his efforts had earned him recognition in the community. Speaking at a luncheon in his honor in Fairfax the previous year, he had described his job as a defense attorney in part as keeping Justice from peeking out from under her blindfold to see who is in court or how close it is to quitting time.

"Now let's look at this thing a little closer," Perkins said to the Fletchers, allowing a hint of excitement in his voice. "As you know, Judge Weston of the District Court, where this case would normally be tried, is a life-long resident of Rappahannock County and he was elected to the bench by the people of the county. He has a good reputation for skill and fairness but the pressures on him can be severe sometimes. Let me remind you of a couple of facts. Judge Weston is up for re-election next year. There has been a rise in juvenile crime in the county in the last couple of years and several members of the Board of Supervisors are on record as thinking that what they call his leniency is part of the problem."

Gerald was impressed with the homework Perkins had done since being engaged to defend Jerry.

"Now, for the clincher," Perkins continued. "The Judge's niece, Caroline, is married to Deputy Jenkins. Thanks to the job our boy Jerry here did on his nose, Jenkins will never be able to steer straight in a high wind again." There was a round of chuckles. "You can imagine the pressure on Weston at family get-togethers these days!"

Perkins waited for the import of his words to settle in before continuing.

"Now those are all facts. Let me add a point of conjecture. If the case against Jerry were cut and dried, I don't think Judge Weston would have had any trouble trying it. It's precisely because he thinks the case is weak that he is afraid of the outcome. And let's face it, Jerry, those officers threw the book at you. They were mad at you and they didn't think through their case. They just wanted to nail you for getting the jump on them, and I believe they exaggerated the charges. Judge Weston suspects that, too, but this way he gets points for being hard on crime by sending your case to the Circuit Court and at the same time he avoids the risk of having you beat the charges on his watch."

The encouragement the Fletchers took from these comments, the relief, was palpable as Perkins concluded his assessment.

"In Circuit Court we're dealing with a judge who is appointed by the state legislature. He doesn't live in the community and his job doesn't depend on the community. If he has ambitions, they lie in Richmond and, let's face it, no one is appointed to the Court of Appeals or the Supreme Court for handing down excessive sentences to juveniles. There's some risk to Jerry in what Judge Weston has done, but I think on the whole it will work in our favor."

CHAPTER 11

On the Tuesday evening following David's guest sermon, Deacon Johnson of the Piedmont congregation telephoned the Williams residence. He wanted to know if there was a convenient time, perhaps later in the week, when he could drop by to meet with James and David. They agreed on Thursday evening, so David had only two days to worry about what the problem might be.

What had he done or said to cause a deacon to call his father and want to see them both? Had he said something in his sermon that wasn't scripturally correct? Had he been too casual or familiar? Maybe it had nothing to do with his sermon. Maybe someone in the Piedmont congregation had seen him in what they considered a compromising position with Sherry. He even prayed about it, but the prayer was more a request for protection than a desire that 'Thy will be done'.

Uncle Marvin would have been quick to see David's fear for what it was: "You can't teach people that the self is evil and then turn around and expect them to think well of themselves. And you sure can't expect them to be able to judge their own actions beyond blind obedience. God forbid that they should ever be creative and then pat themselves on the back for it."

Despite the air of confidence that David exhibited at school and in the pulpit, and the social courage that his faith demanded, he still needed approval more than most people his age, ultimately from his parents. It didn't help that James and Ruth weren't comfortable enough in their own skins to be able to encourage their children in anything beyond the dictates of their faith. Their response to anything the kids did of a creative nature was awkwardness bordering on a chill. When an anxious youngster brought something to them for approval—a school essay or an art project—the typical remark was "Isn't that nice," followed by some suggestion on how it could be improved. Worse still was the suggestion that some other project be tried instead, which to any youngster seven or older meant, 'Give it up, kid. You don't have it.' It was a source of awkwardness between father and son, but David had long ago stopped asking his father for help when he put together guest sermons or talks for young people's meetings.

By the time the door knocker sounded a little after seven o'clock Thursday evening he had resigned himself to some shocking revelation of his faults that would provoke his father's wrath and his mother's sadness.

After a round of family greetings, coffee was arranged, and Deacon Johnson was invited into the small corner room that served as James' office. He was shown to the overstuffed chair in front of the old oak desk and David sat on a kitchen chair that he had brought in earlier for the occasion.

"Well, Deacon," James began. "It's always a pleasure to visit with you when we have the opportunity. The Lord knows we all have such busy schedules. But I understand you have something you want to discuss with us, so please feel free to begin any time."

"Thank you, Pastor," Johnson responded. "I believe I'm bringing news that will please the both of you."

David shifted on his chair and vented the pent-up breath of his apprehension so noticeably that he had to cover it with a cough.

"Excuse me," he said, before pushing back more casually against the rungs of the chair back. So, this wasn't going to be a hanging party after all.

"You must be very proud of your son, Pastor," Deacon Johnson continued. "He's such a fine young man."

"Well, the Lord has been good to him." James didn't take compliments any better than he gave them.

"His sermon last Sunday brought real blessings to a number of our folk," Johnson said and then turned toward David. "Several people spoke to me after the service, David, and I know Deacon Rivers also got a couple of calls."

"Well, thanks very much, Deacon," David responded with a modest smile.

"Now it's not my intention to puff your head up with all this, David, but just to tell you what you probably already know: The Lord works through your preaching."

If he were alone with the deacon, David would have said something about being happy to know that he could be an instrument of the Lord, but with his father in the room it seemed a bit too much. He just deepened his smile toward Johnson, then lowered his head in what might have served as modesty or prayer, but the broken eye contact was also the only form of privacy available to him. He had seen other preachers use it, but it wasn't until he adopted the gesture himself that he discovered the moment of freedom it afforded from the expectant eyes of a congregation.

"Then, Sunday afternoon," Johnson continued, "I received a telephone call from the Widow Pratt, asking me to call on her. You might recollect the Pratts, Pastor. Ethyl's husband Will ran the farm supply and general store over to Madison up until he died about fifteen years back."

"I certainly recognize the name," James answered. In fact, he had bought a keg of nails and some building materials from Pratt and a delay in payment had created some awkwardness. "But I confess I don't believe I've met Mrs. Pratt."

"No matter." Johnson resumed. "They never did have children, you know, and she's there in that big house by herself. Well, she's got Mis' Catlett and old Levi coming in to do chores, but you know what I mean…"

Neither of the Williams men was inclined to the compulsory chatter that accompanies interaction in rural society, but they knew enough to endure it graciously.

"Anyhow, Mis' Pratt is getting on in years, bless her heart, and I was afraid she was going to tell me something about ill health, but nothing could have been further from her mind. She met me at the door, bright and chipper as you please, and walked ahead of me into the parlor where she had arranged some refreshments and a stack of papers. You know, it's right impressive how that woman has taken to managing her husband's affairs. She keeps old Jack Mayhue over to the bank on his toes, let me tell you."

Johnson may have seen the glance between James and David, or he may just have sensed that it was time to get down to business. Either way, he suddenly said, "Anyhow, let me get to why I have come to see you this evening. After telling me how impressed she was with your sermon, David, Mis' Pratt asked me if you planned to go into the ministry. I remembered you telling me one time about your plans for Lynchburg Bible College, so I told her I thought you were."

David smiled, acknowledging the earlier conversation without interrupting. He couldn't explain it, but a knot had begun to form again in his gut, not unlike the feeling a few minutes earlier when he was expecting bad news.

"Well, David, Mis' Pratt has asked me to tell you and your father that she would consider it a privilege to give you whatever financial assistance you might need to attend the bible college of your choice."

Even as he joined his father in expressing surprise and appreciation for such a generous offer, David's unease continued to grow. He tried to ignore it. What could possibly be wrong with someone offering to pick up the tab for his future? But there was a weight on his chest, making him draw short breaths, and the room seemed to be getting warm.

James and the deacon were discussing the offer, how generous Mrs. Pratt was, and considering what might be a convenient time to call on her to express their appreciation. Their voices began to sound muffled. Of course, James and David would have to look into tuition and other costs and do some homework but wasn't it just marvelous how the Lord provides. The more David tried to focus on the conversation the more uneasy he felt, until he began to grow dizzy.

James confessed to some awkwardness about accepting such a gift, but Johnson reassured him with a statement he had almost certainly rehearsed about Williams' generosity and self-sacrifice over the years in the work of the Lord. He had given to others what might have gone to his family and now it was time for someone else to help David realize God's plan for his life.

David was having trouble getting air and he began to feel as though he was going to lose his supper. Managing enough composure to be civil, he excused himself and barely made it to the back yard before doubling over on the lawn. He dry-heaved a couple of times and then projected the contents of his stomach into some dead perennials.

Back inside, James apologized for David's sudden disappearance, suggesting that he had been overwhelmed by Mrs. Pratt's generosity.

"You know how it is with young fellas, they don't like to show their emotions," he explained, reaching over to pour a second cup of coffee for the deacon.

"It's a funny thing about Baptists," Uncle Marvin had said on one of his trips with David. "They're taught that their bodies are the temple of the Holy Spirit, but then they never learn to listen to their bodies. In fact, they're drilled into believing that the things of the flesh are evil and the needs of the body are temporal. And woe to anybody who would ever betray God's divine guidance by getting help from a shrink. So they live in a temple that has bats in the belfry and sewage in the basement and they call it home. If that's not a formula for neuroses, I don't know what is."

Until Mrs. Pratt's offer, David had succeeded, for the most part, in keeping the question of his future at a comfortable distance. The assumption in his family and among those who knew of his church work was that he was going to go to bible college. Going along with that assumption had taken the pressure off a subject of major concern to most of his contemporaries. At the level of casual conversation, his future was a done deal and that had lulled him into a degree of complacency with respect to any particular course of action.

In fact, there hadn't been enough immediacy in the plan to keep his mind from wandering beyond the ministry. In the pulpit, of course, he experienced the power of spiritual leadership and a strong pull to the ministry. But in class he found himself thinking about going to university, studying science or economics, and at half time in a game they were winning he would fantasize about a football scholarship, maybe even a professional sports career.

Others in his class were well into the process of applying to colleges or looking for jobs but, with this vague presumption of a career in the ministry, he had not until tonight faced up to the fact that at some point he was going to have to make a decision. Now that decision was placed squarely in front of him, wrapped in expectations.

* * * * *

Friday after school he gave Sherry a lift as usual but this time he didn't take her straight home. He hadn't been able to pull himself together since the conversation with Deacon Johnson and, while he worried about upsetting her with his doubts about going into the ministry, he needed to talk to somebody. There was no way he would risk admitting his uncertainty to an authority figure, especially his father, but Sherry actually seemed to like a bit of uncertainty in him. She said it showed sensitivity, which was apparently a good thing.

"Do you mind if we take a little drive?" he asked.

She could see that something was on his mind so, keeping things light, she said, "No, of course not," and didn't push for an explanation.

He turned up Rock Mills Road and headed out across the rolling farmland. Fifteen minutes later they were sitting on a rock by the edge of the Rush River. David had trouble making conversation and he focused intermittently on throwing stones at the fall leaves that drifted downstream across the old swimming hole.

Finally, Sherry said, "Is something wrong, David?" and as quickly as if her question had given him permission to speak, he asked, "Would you be disappointed if I didn't become a minister?" He continued to look out across the water.

"What a crazy question," she replied. "Of course not. And where did such an idea come from anyhow?"

He turned toward her now and told her about Deacon Johnson's visit and the Widow Pratt's offer. After hesitating a moment, he decided to tell her about his reaction, about needing to escape from the room and then being sick.

"It was like I couldn't breathe," David continued, embarrassed by the memory.

"But what was it about the meeting that did that to you? It was a generous offer, wasn't it?"

"Sure it was—is" he corrected. "It's just that I don't know if I can accept it."

"Of course you can. That woman wants you to have the money. She believes in you and she believes in the Gospel. Otherwise, she wouldn't have made the offer."

"No, that's not what I mean." David took another pass at explaining the situation without coming right out with how he really felt. "I mean I don't know if I can become a minister."

"Now come on, David James." She used his full name when she pretended to scold him. The effect was either cuddly or sarcastic depending on the circumstances and this time the sarcasm was cutting-edge clear. "Do you mean to tell me that you think the program may be too difficult?"

"No, of course not." David's voice was higher and louder now, his frustration showing. "OK, here it is." He brought his voice back under control and after a deep breath he said, almost sadly, "I don't think I want to be a minister."

"Right, and what's the problem?" Sherry knew full well the kind of pressures that David had faced in the direction of a church calling, but she couldn't think of any other way to tell him how she felt.

After a few moments he took his eyes off the river to look in her direction. They were filled with tears, but he was smiling.

"Thank you."

She reached over and slapped him on the back of the head.

"You men can be so dense."

CHAPTER 12

"All rise. The Twentieth Judicial Circuit Court is now in session, Judge Wallace T. Bickford presiding."

Deputy Settles stood stiffly with his papers in one hand until the judge took his seat and then added, "Be seated."

Setting a thermos and a cup to one side of the desk, the judge proceeded to arrange his papers for the morning session.

"What have we got this morning, Mis' Carol?" he asked in a light-hearted tone. Bickford, of course, knew the caseload for the day, but this was his signature opening statement, his message to those present that he was not troubled by the weight of office.

The Clerk of the Court stood and spoke clearly and matter-of-factly, "Case number CR66000137-00, Your Honor, a pretrial hearing for the Commonwealth of Virginia v. Gerald Fletcher Junior." She knew the routine, too, and she spread her reading of the charges out long enough for Bickford to finish pouring the first cup of coffee from his thermos.

The judge's circuit included three counties. He spent two days a week on the home bench in Warrenton, adjudicating an array of civil and criminal cases from Fauquier County. On the other three days he rode the circuit, two days to Leesburg for the Loudon court, and once a week to the village of Washington to preside over the much smaller Rappahannock court.

Judge Bickford had a soft spot for Rappahannock County. He was eighth-generation Virginian but he was also eighth-generation Francis Thornton Valley. Much of the old family estate had been divided and sold, but the main house still stood about five miles south of Sperryville, surrounded by two hundred acres of corn and pasture and backed up against the lower edge of the Blue Ridge and the Park. His brother's oldest son ran the place now, but regular family get-togethers kept everyone in touch, and in love with Bluemont.

The Clerk continued, "As Your Honor will have noted, this case has been certified for adjudication in this court by His Honor Terrence Weston of the Rappahannock District Court. The Bill of Indictment and Judge Weston' certification are Documents 1 and 2, respectively, in Your Honor's case file."

The gallery of the courtroom was empty except for Faith and Gerald, who were seated in the first row of wooden chairs, directly behind the defense table where Jerry sat nervously with Perkins. In contrast to Perkins' confident air, the defendant leaned on the arms of his chair, staring down at his hands, clasped and fidgeting in front of him.

Commonwealth's Attorney Charles Mathews occupied the prosecutor's table on the opposite side of the room and they all faced Judge Bickford whose desk, flanked by the Stars and Stripes and Virginia's colors, was on a raised platform behind a low wooden partition running the width of the room. To his right was the desk occupied by the Clerk of the Court, and to his left was the witness chair. Large windows on both sides of the chamber admitted bright sunlight that highlighted the portraits of past judges hanging about the walls. The room smelled of old wood and new paint and its sparse furnishings and heavy colonial molding did little to soften the sounds of people and process. The oak floor creaked when anyone moved about the room and voices resonated with authority.

The judge looked down in the direction of the defense table.

"Good morning, Mr. Perkins."

"Good morning, Your Honor."

"I haven't seen you in one of my courtrooms for some time, Mr. Perkins. Too busy with cases in the big city, are we?"

"No, sir, Your Honor. Just the luck of the draw." He never knew what sensitivities lay back of Bickford's seemingly light-hearted comments, so it was best to deflect them politely.

It was unlikely that Bickford recognized the defendant as the grandson of the last man to care for his family's herds in the summer pasture. Too much time and too many faces had gone by for that, but the history was in his blood. The family's version of the events leading up to the establishment of the Park differed from that of the general public but then, as Grandma Bickford used to put it, most historians were the scribes for latter-day carpetbaggers anyhow.

Until her dying day, Grandma Bickford told anyone who would listen how difficult things had been for the family in those days. It was the middle of the Depression and, with the loss of the mountain grazing, bottomland that once produced hay had to be used for pasture. That meant buying hay for winter feeding, and it meant hiring more men to tend the cattle during summer months. The family had had to cut back from three hundred cows to two hundred. They had hired Charlottesville lawyers and fought the expropriation long enough to get a good price out of Richmond but, despite the price, Grandma Bickford said she was almost reduced to selling the family crystal to pay those distasteful characters. She was heard to say on numerous occasions, "Why, it's a wonder we were able to help out the Cowans down at Etlan at all, taking those two hundred acres off their hands before the bank could steal it."

As for the mountain people who didn't own land, the feeling was that if the Government insisted on helping them resettle, that was New Deal foolishness and not to be helped, at least not until the next election.

The shift to more farm hands and suppliers in the lowlands meant that Old Man Bickford developed a more extensive network of local business acquaintances. Mrs. Bickford thought it was disgraceful how her husband would socialize with merchants and tradespeople or come home late with some stranger he had invited for dinner. But when he parlayed that into a seat in the State legislature she didn't mind so much. There was talk of the State Senate and maybe Washington, but certain of the duties of office appealed to Bickford more than others and he had succumbed to liver failure before the end of his second term.

"Thank you, Mis' Carol," the judge continued. "Now, before we begin let me just say a word or two." He had indeed prepared for this case and had seen some potential problems. "The charges being brought in this case are serious, but it's an unusual case in that we have a young man under the age of 18 being brought into circuit court, a young man who I understand is facing his first criminal charges."

Bickford looked at Jerry, but there was no hint of warmth in his glance.

"I have two purposes in conducting this hearing. First, I want to satisfy myself of a prima facie case for the charges; and second, I want to establish any specific procedures that will be necessary to ensure that we respect the interests of minors in the trial itself. Are there any questions?"

Neither attorney had noted anything of concern in the judge's remarks and neither had any questions.

"Fine, then. Mr. Mathews, would you begin, please. I want to hear your summary of the events leading to the charges before the court and then an outline of the case you intend to present."

"Thank you, Your Honor," Mathews replied.

In the few moments while Mathews was arranging his papers to begin, Perkins turned to Jerry, who had tensed to the point that his knuckles had lost their color. Perkins bent toward his client's ear as though to consult with him.

"Listen to these guys," he whispered. "You can understand why people say that the king's English is better preserved in the Virginia Piedmont than anywhere else in the empire." He pronounced empire with a long soft a where the i should be, and a silent r. Jerry smiled, but any relief he felt was short-lived.

"Your Honor, the charges in this case are indeed serious, as you have noted," Mathews began as he stood and came out from behind his table.

He was in his first term as Commonwealth's Attorney for the county, having grown up in nearby Madison County, attended the University of Virginia Law School, and then practiced in the county for more than ten years. He was on a first-name basis with most people on both sides of the courtroom and in the Sheriff's department, but now he spoke in the slow deliberate style that took maximum advantage of his office and of the acoustics in the room.

"These charges stem from an altercation on the evening of November 12, 1965, between the accused and, initially, one other minor, in which the accused inflicted injuries on the other youth to an extent requiring hospitalization, including an overnight stay."

Hospitalization and overnight stay are both defining terms for the severity of violent crime under Virginia law, and Mathews was careful to articulate them clearly. As he spoke, he had gradually moved across the courtroom to position himself between the judge and Jerry. Now, he began to reinforce each statement of fact against Jerry with accusatory gestures in his direction with a handful of papers, at the same time engaging the judge with earnest eyes.

"When two uniformed officers of the Sheriff's Department intervened to break up this altercation, Your Honor, the accused turned his rage on them and inflicted injuries on the officers requiring emergency treatment by Doc Carson at the clinic here in town."

Mathews paused to let the facts concerning the defendant's behavior register with the judge. His manner would have had more effect on a jury than on a seasoned judge, but Bickford was not beyond appreciating a bit of courtroom theatrics if he happened to share the sentiment.

"Since the operation of a vehicle was not involved in this case, no sobriety test was conducted at the scene, Your Honor, but the accused did exhibit a lack of balance and slurred, halting speech."

Perkins murmured something Jerry couldn't understand, scribbled a note in the margin of his prepared remarks, and underlined it.

"The arresting officers noted the smell of beer on his person," Mathews continued, "and there were beer cans scattered about the scene."

Mathews concluded his account of the facts that led to the charges and moved back to his table. Rearranging his notes, he picked up another sheet and continued. "In reporting the events of that night, Your Honor, the Sheriff's Department noted, in particular, the viciousness with which the accused attacked the other youth and his flagrant disregard for the officers of the law who intervened. The case we intend to present to the court will prove this viciousness and this disregard. We will call as witnesses the arresting officers, attending medical personnel, the minor who was the victim, and other youths who witnessed the altercation."

"Thank you, Mr. Mathews." Judge Bickford put down the fountain pen with which he had made notes while Mathews spoke. "I have a couple of questions for clarification if you please."

"Most certainly, Your Honor"

"Were the accused and the other named minor the only two involved in the altercation?"

"No, Your Honor. There were four youths actively engaged in the fight, and a number of others looking on."

"And young Mr. Fletcher is the only one charged?"

"That is correct, Your Honor."

"What of the others on his side of the conflict?"

"There weren't any others, Your Honor. Mr. Fletcher acted alone."

"And by that you mean that Mr. Fletcher was fighting three opponents at the same time?"

"That is correct, Your Honor. One of the other youths was also injured in the fight but his representatives have requested that the charges for those injuries be dropped."

"The indictment makes no reference to weapons, Mr. Mathews. Were any used in the altercation?"

"Yes, Your Honor. The defendant did use a stout stick during the fight, but it was not used to inflict any of the injuries to which the charges are related."

Perkins had been adamant in his instruction to Jerry before the trial that he remain silent and calm whatever went on. With this talk of the stick he took from Dodson as a weapon, the only way Jerry could sit calmly was to imagine Mathews in his rifle sights.

"Thank you, Mr. Mathews. And tell me, does the Commonwealth acknowledge any provocation for Mr. Fletcher's actions?"

"None that would explain the nature of the response, Your Honor. As far as we have been able to ascertain, there was an exchange of crude remarks but nothing that would appear to have gone beyond normal schoolyard banter."

Unnoticed by Mathews, Perkins drew a dense black line under one of the points on his sheet of prepared notes.

"Thank you, Mr. Mathews. Very helpful." Then, as if as an afterthought, Bickford added, "Oh, one final point for clarification, please. The Bill of Indictment does not state how the Sheriff's office was notified of the altercation. Would you advise the court as to how the deputies managed to arrive on the scene while the fight was still going on?"

It seemed like a simple question.

Mathews replied in a straightforward manner.

"Your Honor, the Sheriff's Department received a telephone complaint from a resident of Sperryville whose house backs onto the yard where the altercation took place. Mrs. Hank Lawford had watched the situation develop from the time she first heard the boys in the yard."

"Well, if that's the case, Mr. Mathews, you will appreciate my puzzlement at the fact that Mis' Lawford does not appear on the list of witnesses for the prosecution."

The Commonwealth's Attorney showed the first hint of fluster, a slight reddening of his cheeks and a delayed response. When she was interviewed, Mrs. Lawson hadn't been able to corroborate the version of events the prosecution planned to present, so Mathews had decided not to call her as a witness.

"Your Honor, Mrs. Lawson has been under a lot of pressure caring for her ailing husband these last few months. We felt that these proceedings would impose undue stress on her, and the case was sufficiently strong without her testimony."

"We shall learn in due course the strength of your case, Mr. Mathews, but I thank you for your enlightenment."

As Mathews took his seat, he hoped it was just Bickford's style that had rattled him and not some misgiving on the judge's part as to the case he was about to try.

"Now, Mr. Perkins. If there were any points of fact in the Prosecution's description of the events leading up to the charges that you intend to challenge, you may signal that intent, but I caution you not to embark on any posturing or re-interpretation. We are engaged in summarizing facts at this time. What I am mainly interested in hearing from you is the outline of the case you intend to present.

"Thank you, Your Honor." Perkins stood as he continued, "In the interest of the Court's time, I'll come straight to the point: Defense is prepared to stipulate as to the following facts concerning the events that led to the charges against my client. First, the Defendant did consume an unspecified quantity of an alcoholic beverage on the night in question. Second, the Defendant did engage in an altercation with the injured minor named in the indictment. And third, the Defendant did inflict the documented injuries on the named minor and on two officers of the Sheriff's Department."

Perkins paused and placed the first sheet of his prepared notes face down on the table beside him. Then, without referring to the remaining notes in his hand, he looked directly at Judge Bickford and moved toward the bench.

"However, Your Honor, there are two alleged facts cited by the Prosecution which we deny categorically and which we will prove to be false in our defense: First, that there was no provocation that would account for the Defendant's actions and second, that the Defendant knowingly turned his anger on the officers who attempted to intervene.

"I would also like to introduce several additional facts surrounding the events of November the 12th, Your Honor. The first is that the altercation at issue actually began several minutes earlier than heretofore acknowledged, when the Defendant was subjected to an unprovoked attack by the alleged victim. The Defendant avoided the punch thrown by the other minor and knocked him down in a defensive maneuver. As the Defendant walked away from the scene, the assailant and two other minors armed themselves and called after the Defendant.

"It was at this time that a series of vile accusations of criminal sexual conduct within the Defendant's family were thrown at the Defendant, with the conscious intent of provoking a violent response."

"Now just a minute, Mr. Perkins." Bickford was visibly annoyed. "I don't know what they call it where you come from, but in my court 'vile' is a characterization and 'conscious intent to provoke' is a judgment. I don't recall asking for either from you and I caution you that I will not tolerate either from you. Do I make myself clear?"

Perkins was taken aback by the strength of the rebuke. He knew he had been sailing close to the wind, but he had expected to have his tiller adjusted a little more gently at this early stage of the proceedings.

"Yes, Your Honor, perfectly clear."

"Then you may continue." The judge broke eye contact and returned to his note-taking position. Perkins resumed, with a hint of deference.

"The Defendant tried on three occasions to get the others to cease their taunting, Your Honor, but as we will show, they did not, instead, increasing the severity of their accusations until the Defendant did indeed lose control and respond physically. It is because the Defendant knows he should have walked away, that he will plead guilty to the charge of disorderly conduct."

Perkins let that fact rest on the judge's mind for a moment and then continued.

"When the altercation began, Your Honor, the Defendant faced three assailants, each carrying a weapon capable of inflicting grievous injury. I don't believe that Your Honor would consider it a characterization to suggest that my client was fully preoccupied with the altercation from that moment forward."

Bickford glanced at Perkins to be sure that there wasn't any sarcasm in his face and, satisfied that it was an objective statement, he made no comment.

"Incidentally, Your Honor, the weapon to which the Prosecution referred earlier was in fact first used by one of those assailants and was knocked from his hand by the accused in a defensive maneuver."

Perkins took a moment at this point to walk back to his table and look at his notes, turning several sheets over to find his place. Straightening the lapels of his jacket with both hands, he moved back into the center of the room, established eye contact with the judge, and continued.

"Your Honor, there is one important fact concerning this incident that has not yet been recorded." Perkins had set the stage well, and he was rewarded with a look of surprise on Bickford's face when he said, "This altercation took place in the dark." After a moment, he continued, "That's correct, Your Honor. It took place some two hours after sunset. There was virtually no natural light at the scene, and the building that houses the general store and residences at that location blocked the light from streetlights on Route 522. To all intents and purposes, Your Honor, the altercation took place in the dark."

"Duly noted, Mr. Perkins. Please move along."

Perkins recognized that Bickford was making a point with him. No big city attorney was going to come into his courtroom and presume to get away with any theatrics.

"Of course, Your Honor. I ask the Court's forgiveness. There are only two additional points I wish to have the Court take note of. The first is that the Sheriff's Deputies approached the accused from behind, and they did not identify themselves."

The judge looked up at Perkins and then, incredulous, turned his stare toward the Commonwealth's Attorney.

"The second is rather more of a question, Your Honor. Why did two officers of the law, with over four hundred pounds between them and two recent physical fitness awards, choose to end the confrontation with Mr. Fletcher by a blow to the head with a nightstick that rendered him unconscious and resulted in a concussion?"

"Mr. Perkins, the Sheriff's Department is not on trial here."

"But, Your Honor, they have the temerity to conclude that this boy was drunk because he couldn't walk straight after being knocked unconscious?"

"That's enough, Mr. Perkins."

"Your Honor, they didn't even arrange for any medical attention. It wasn't until his parents took him to Front Royal the next day that his condition was diagnosed."

By now the judge was furious.

"Mr. Perkins, you'd better be finished. You're lucky there isn't a jury in this room, or I'd skin you alive."

Bickford took a moment to recompose himself before continuing.

"Now unless you have any additional facts of an admissible nature, I suggest you proceed to summarize your case."

Perkins showed enough deference in his posture to put the judge at ease and began his concluding remarks.

"In summary, Your Honor, the Defendant will plead guilty to the charges of drinking underage and disorderly conduct. He will plead not guilty to assault and battery and not guilty to assaulting an officer. The case we present will show that the Defendant was among a number of youths engaged in a Saturday evening drinking party that got out of control and that the Defendant, in a misguided defense of his family's honor, engaged in a fight with three other youths. We will then show that the intensity of the Defendant's aggression was due entirely to the fact that he was coping with three armed adversaries. In the middle of this one-sided fight he could not possibly have been expected to take the time to ascertain that those attempting to restrain him, from behind, in the dark, without identifying themselves, were persons other than adversaries, let alone officers of the law." Without further comment, Perkins turned and walked back to his table.

"I have only one question for you, Mr. Perkins. Who is this Dr. Cynthia Jefferson you plan to call as a defense witness?"

"Your Honor, Dr. Jefferson is married to Hank Lawford. She retains her maiden name for purposes of her profession. She is an orthopedic surgeon in Culpeper."

"Well, that's very progressive of her, but what has she to do with this case?"

Again, Perkins had set the stage well.

"Your Honor, it was Dr. Jefferson who called the Sheriff's office to report the altercation."

There was complete silence as Bickford absorbed this information and put his thoughts together. Then, shaking his head, he said, "At this time, ladies and gentlemen, I am going to recess this hearing. Mis' Carol, I assume we have some time available on next week's docket?"

"Yes, Your Honor. Would ten o'clock be satisfactory?"

"Ten it is," Bickford said. "We'll resume at 10 AM next Thursday, and I want to see the commonwealth's attorney and defense counsel in my chambers before that, at nine o'clock. Is that clear?"

Both attorneys acknowledged the instruction and Bickford concluded, "This hearing is adjourned," and dropped his gavel.

CHAPTER 13

Marvin Williams always took a break after his mid-day meal. It was a holdover from his years in the tropics, and he welcomed it each day like an old friend. He called it his siesta, although he was just as likely to read as he was to nap.

When the phone rang, he reluctantly set down his current edition of The Foreign Service Journal and reached for the receiver.

"Hey, Uncle Marvin. It's David."

A call from his nephew was one of the few interruptions of his quiet time that he would not have viewed with ambivalence or outright resentment.

"Hello, kid. How are you doing?"

"I'm fine, thanks. Well, sort of. There's some stuff going on these days."

"And since you don't call me very often, I'm guessing that whatever's going on may be unusual, too."

He saw something of himself in young David—the need to question, the unwillingness to take things at face value. And his encouragement of this curiosity had never had to be tempered with the realities of being a parent himself.

"Yeah. Actually, I was calling to see if I could come down and maybe hang out at your place for a day or two."

Marvin began to put the pieces together.

"You're probably not calling from home, then, are you?"

"No, I'm at a friend's. I thought I'd see if it was OK with you first, and then I'd tell Mom."

When David had asked to make a long-distance call on the Atkins line, Sherry's father had shown his distaste at being put in the middle of another family's business, but Sherry had come to the rescue.

"Daddy, this is important," she had said in that firm tone that daughters learn to use with such effect on their fathers.

Marvin was speaking again.

"I guess I'm in my brother's bad books deep enough already that a little conspiracy won't make any difference. Sure. Come on down."

"That's great. Thanks."

"Madge is away visiting her family these days, but we can manage. When were you thinking of coming?"

"How about sometime in the next couple of hours?"

* * * * *

Two weeks had passed since David told his father of his wish to go to university instead of bible college. James hadn't quoted scripture and gone off on him the way David expected. Instead, there had been a long silence during which he shuffled through papers on his desk or stared out the window. Eventually, he had asked, "Have you prayed about this?"

"Yes, sir. More than about anything else I can remember." David had opened his mouth as if to continue, but he wasn't sure, if he did start to explain, that he could keep from crying. So, he said nothing.

He had so much wanted a clear message from God. He had so much wanted to choose a path that would please James. But in the end, all he had to go on was the sense of being alive when he was chasing down the elusive bits of some research project at school and the constriction in his chest each time he thought of a future behind the pulpit.

A couple of times James had started to say something, but instead, he just cleared his throat and continued to arrange things on his desk. Then, without looking at his son, he had pushed his chair back and slowly stood.

"I guess that's it then." There had been disappointment in his voice, but something else, too: a shortness that hinted at anger.

With David's assurance that he had prayed long and hard about his future, James couldn't challenge the decision directly. But he was sure that, if David had truly sought God's will in a spirit of obedience, the Lord would have guided him toward bible college and the ministry. The Devil used scripture for his own purposes, so he certainly wasn't above using prayer. Right here in James's own house, he had led David to use prayer to protect himself and his decision. Those were grounds for righteous wrath if ever there were any, but this wasn't the time. Anger might just strengthen David's resolve. All those years of teaching and guidance, wasted, gone.

With self-pity as the catalyst, his anger had almost fully dissolved into sadness as he spoke again, "I'm sorry that the Lord hasn't found you fit for his service," he said. "That's a big disappointment to me." Then, he had turned and walked out of the room.

* * * *

David pulled into Marvin's yard about four in the afternoon, as his uncle was loading bags of feed into the back of the pickup.

"Good timing," Marvin called out. "Put your shit boots on and you can give me a hand with the afternoon feeding."

So much for any awkwardness David might have anticipated on his arrival. "OK, I'll be right with you."

He had left a pair of work boots in a locker in the barn the last time he helped Marvin. Turning them over, he gave them a good shake to dislodge any rodent nests, then put them on and returned to the yard. A couple of minutes later he held the gate open as the pickup pulled into the pasture, then climbed back in the passenger side.

"We did a final round of vaccinating and castrating a week or so back," Marvin said as they headed up a dirt track toward the row of feed troughs. "So just keep an eye out for any calves that might look out of sorts."

Cows had begun to move toward them from both sides, their calves darting ahead or holding back in their amusing mix of energy and apprehension.

"Everybody looks fine from here," David said. "How many calves did you have this year?"

"Forty-three, total. One stillborn, and I lost a couple to that nasty ice storm back in February. Putting calfsicles in a tub of warm water and hoping for the best is not my favorite part of this job."

"No, that's got to be tough."

"McTavish did a good job for me again this year. We won't be preg checking for another month or two, but he seems to have next year's crop under control, too.

"That's three or four years you've had him now, right?"

"Four years this summer. He's certainly earned his keep. If I decide to shorten the calving period, I'll have to think about a second bull. But that's a lot of extra work and worry. For now, I'm happy the way things are."

The casual exchange continued as they poured feed into the troughs and watched the cows mill around before settling into their feeding routine.

"So tell me, what kind of stuff would send you and your toothbrush down this way on such short notice?"

"Well, as you might have guessed, my old man and I had a blowup."

"That's progress. It used to be just him blowing up."

"Yeah, but he's my old man, Marvin. It's not right."

"Good god, man, what planet are you from? Father-and-son is a two-person deal. Father isn't a get-out-of-jail card if he's fucking up."

David struggled for a moment between relief at Marvin's support and the instinct to defend his father.

"What did you do, anyhow – track mud on the carpet?"

"Come on, Marvin. This is serious. I was helping unload a truck at his Huntly job this morning and I lost my grip on a window. When it fell, a couple of the panes broke, and he exploded. I guess I shouted back at him, but all I said was that it was heavy, and it slipped.

"He said, 'How dare you talk back to me,' and grabbed my shirt as if he was going to hit me. I pushed him back – I thought I was just trying to get free but, when I looked, my hand was on his throat. We just stood there for a moment staring at each other. We were both really mad. But then it was like we were embarrassed. We let go of each other, and I just walked away. I hitch-hiked back to town. Then I went to Sherry's house and decided to call you."

They arrived back in the barnyard as David finished speaking. Marvin turned the key off but made no move to get out of the truck, instead, leaning back and resting his arm on the steering wheel.

"So, the old bull has a challenger, huh? Well, well."

"I told him a couple of weeks ago that I wanted to go to university instead of bible college. We haven't talked since, except to be civil."

"What did he say when you told him that?"

"Not much. Just that he was disappointed."

"And he's held out this long, huh? Pretty impressive."

"What are you talking about?"

"Let me ask you a question. If you thought you had a direct line on God's will and you'd worked for 17 years to deliver your first-born to the ministry, how would you feel if that kid tossed it all over in favor of intellectual curiosity? Disappointed? Yeah, for sure. But that would just be the top layer. And my brother is not inclined to self-reflection, so the next layer sure as hell wasn't wondering what he might have done to make you go wrong. As far as he's concerned, what you did boils down to disrespect for him and his God, plain and simple. How the hell did he hold out for two weeks?"

"But that's not it at all, Marvin. It has nothing to do with respect."

"Don't try to tell him that. His world is black and white, and you came out on the wrong side of this one."

"But I can't do it. I can't go into the ministry. My heart's not in it."

"I know that. I've watched you struggling for the last couple of years."

"About the ministry? I don't remember us even talking about it."

"No, not the ministry specifically, but the whole issue of believing versus thinking. And, at least for the full-blown Baptist version of the ministry, you have to be a believer. I don't mean whether or not you believe there's some greater power in the universe; I mean a dot-the-i's, cross-the-t's believer. The literal interpretation of Scripture. You've been trying to be both a believer and a thinker for a while now. Not working very well, is it?"

"I keep thinking there has to be a way."

"Well, if you ever figure that one out there'll be a line at your door, you can bet on that. As far as I've been able to tell, a person is either a thinker, who lets belief stand in temporarily until he has the evidence to confirm or reject an idea, or he's a believer who, when push comes to shove, relegates thought to the role of proving what he's already decided is true. Is that what you want – to limit your thinking to hamster-wheel bullshit like how many angels can fit on the head of a pin, or to let yourself wonder about whether angels even exist?

David shrugged, "It's not really baseball if you start on second base, is it?"

"Exactly. Taking your turn at bat; the outs, the wild pitches – you avoid all that risk by starting on second, for sure, but so what? Hell, you might as well take the dog with you and stroll home. We're not all Babe Ruth, but shouldn't we at least take a turn at bat?"

An easy silence filled the cab of the truck. Marvin had said what needed to be said. David had found reassurance that his growing doubts and uncertainty weren't just a sign of his own weakness.

There were a few chores left to do – refuel the tractor, close up the chicken coop, put fresh water down for the barn cats. David told Marvin to go ahead into the house; he'd finish up, and he moved through the remaining tasks in a more relaxed state than he had known for some time. Analogies aside, the idea sat well with him: Thinking was more important. Acknowledging that didn't fix things like making peace with his father or deciding what to study, but it would help.

As he made his way toward the house, he thought about the college applications he'd put together in recent weeks and made a mental note to take care of several loose ends on the Virginia Tech application.

When he came through the back door into the kitchen, Marvin had already washed up and taken a beer from the fridge. He was sitting at the table with the day's mail in front of him.

"There are a couple of Nehis in the fridge. Help yourself."

"Sounds good. I'll be back in a minute."

After he dropped his kit bag at the foot of the stairs and washed up, David sat opposite Marvin and took a sip from a cold grape soda.

"Bills and ads," Marvin said. "That's all there ever is in the mailbox, but every day I walk across the road and check just the same. Wonder what it is I'm looking for."

"Come on, now. With all the weird and wonderful places you've had a mailbox, there had to have been at least a few items of interest."

"Yeah, I suppose... I'll tell you, though, the most stressful was always the notice for my next overseas posting. If the next two years of your life could just as easily be spent in Kampala as London, a lot of hours went into wondering which it was going to be."

"What was your favorite posting?"

"I wouldn't be able to pick one place. There were several that I liked for different reasons: Nairobi, Kuala Lumpur, Beirut..."

To David these were names on a map, mental keyholes to mysterious worlds, but they rolled off Marvin's tongue as if they were old friends he'd had a drink with on the way home. It was an intimacy that captured David's imagination in a way he didn't yet understand.

"I'd have to include Marseilles, as well," Marvin added.

"Not Paris?"

"Hell, no. Parisians are a snooty bunch. But the south of France, that's different."

"How so?"

"Provence has a rhythm, a timelessness all its own. Life comes together there somehow. Whatever the job is, it gets done, but not at the expense of everything else. And the Cezannes of this world were really onto something. The light on a summer day in Provence is magical. It's not the stand-at-attention, sundial kind of light that wears you out, but a presence. Where else in the world could you find vibrant pastels?"

"That sounds amazing."

"And as incredible as all that is, my Provence was something different." Marvin paused, and when he spoke again, his voice was softer, reflective. "My Provence was a gentle rain on a late October day. Muted colors, fields gleaned and resting. It was mist in the lane and a fire in the hearth."

David smiled. "That's starting to sound like you shared it with someone."

Marvin acknowledged the comment with a smile of his own. "Maybe someday, when your ideals have been knocked around a little, I'll tell you a story."

"I'll do my best to get ready for that," David said, finishing the last of his soda.

"Those are small bottles. You'd better have the other one."

As David stood and made his way to the fridge, he concurred in the change of subject by asking, "Your last posting was to New Delhi, right?"

"That's right."

"If you don't mind me asking, why'd you quit? I mean you obviously enjoyed the work, the travel. You had some interesting assignments and then, BAM, finished."

"It was the greatest job in the world, most of the time. But like any job worth doing, there's always the risk that you'll get caught crossways between what you value and what the boss wants you to do."

"That's got a familiar ring to it."

"Right. Well, most of the time you just buck up and get on with it, but there's a limit and I reached mine in Delhi."

"I'd like to hear about that if you're up to telling me."

"Sure. Have you ever heard of the PL 480?"

"Something to do with developing countries, right?"

"Right. These days they're also calling it the Food for Peace Program. The agricultural products the US gives to developing countries every year under this program save thousands of lives. The first year I was in Delhi, that program was part of my responsibilities and it accounted for about forty percent of all the grain consumed in the whole country."

"That's pretty impressive. It doesn't sound like something you'd quit your job over though. What am I missing?"

"Of course not, smart ass. But stick around for a minute. Food for Peace isn't entirely a selfless humanitarian gesture. It's a good way to get rid of the huge surpluses that build up in this country because of farm subsidies. Also, a few shiploads of grain or milk powder can make you some friends when you need them. Both are perfectly reasonable parts of foreign policy."

"OK. That takes a bit of the shine off the apple, but so far, so good."

"Let me give you two more ingredients and then I'll bake the pie. First, we ask governments that receive PL 480 commodities to take some of what they would normally have spent for those products in international markets and invest it in their own agriculture. Fair enough, right? To reduce future dependence on food imports."

"That makes sense."

"OK, and that commitment is made in writing in a Memorandum of Understanding with the government.

"Second," he continued, "think about the politics of the South Asia region at the time. It was the height of the love affair between India and the Soviet Union, and we were cozy with Pakistan. The Indians were getting everything from T-55 tanks to MiG 21s from the Soviets, and our friends in Pakistan weren't happy about that. In fact, the Indians had a good deal; they were getting what they wanted from both superpowers: food from us and arms from the Soviets. Now, are you ready for the pie?"

"I guess so. That's sure an interesting bunch of ingredients."

"It would normally have been my job to draft the Memorandum of Understanding to be signed with the government. But one morning I was called, with the others who worked on PL 480, to an unusual meeting chaired by the ambassador. It seemed weird that the military attaché was sitting beside him, but then the clincher: we were handed copies of an MOU that had already been delivered to India's Ministry of Foreign Affairs."

"Sounding a bit spooky, Marvin."

"Never mind all the wherefores and whereases; what it said was that instead of putting the PL 480 money into agricultural development, India would use it to invest in heavy industries and start to produce its own military equipment. Oh, and by the way, our friends at Lockheed and General Motors will be happy to lend you a hand."

David looked perplexed. "So, we wanted to use food to make tanks. Was that it?"

"In a way it was ingenious," Marvin continued, "In one fell swoop that agreement could have marked the end of the Soviet's largest market for military equipment, given the US an inside track on Indian military strategy and given the Pakistanis a chance to relax for five years while India figured out what it was doing. It set Tata and Hindustan Industries up with massive new investments and it set the stage for new joint ventures for US military giants. What a coup, right?"

David nodded, though he knew something was still coming.

"Two problems," Marvin concluded. "First, the Indians weren't that fucking stupid and, second, it proved that no one really cared about the 60 million small farm families who would be left to eke out a living with primitive technology.

"So that was it. I didn't like the big boys capturing something that was supposed to alleviate hunger and poverty. And I was embarrassed that my government could think that the Indians would ever give up their ability to play both sides of the power game. I submitted my resignation the next day."

Marvin took the last sip of his beer and stared absently at the top of the table.

"There's a big world out there, kid. Definitely worth a look. It's not all warm and fuzzy, but don't be discouraged by a few bad apple stories. There's a lot to do, and it can be a fun trip."

CHAPTER 14

The commonwealth's attorney and Jerry's defense council climbed the stairs of the courthouse and made their way to Judge Bickford's chambers at the appointed hour. Bickford had also just arrived and was seated behind the spacious oak desk to one side of the room when they knocked.

"Enter."

"Good morning, Your Honor."

Mathews closed the door behind them, and both attorneys stood in silence awaiting instruction as Bickford finished removing papers from his briefcase and arranging them on his desk. The smell of fresh paint in the room was tempered with the sweet musk the old Virginia Reports books that lined the wall of built-in shelves opposite the judge's desk. Time and light had worked the thick backs of the volumes into a pallet of creams, ochres and browns. The smudges and frays of use had given each volume a distinct identity but together the collection created a mottled wash of color across the wall that, in the morning sunlight, brought an impressionist's warmth to the otherwise austere space.

"Sit down, gentlemen," Bickford said, gesturing to the two straight-backed wooden chairs in front of his desk. Then he began to speak in a measured tone that made Perkins and Mathews uneasy.

"For the next few minutes, I'm going to assume that I am dealing with reasonable men and you, gentlemen, are going to make the same assumption."

He fixed their stare with his own long enough to make sure they weren't going to interrupt him and then continued.

"Our conversation is not part of the court record and, make a note of this, gentlemen: it is not to be shared in your office coffee cliques. However, any understandings reached in this room will be respected on pain of my eternal wrath. Do I make myself clear?"

The two attorneys shifted uneasily. Conduct in judges' chambers was governed by well-established rules and the fact that Bickford had restated them and imbued them with his personal threat was disturbing.

"Of course, Your Honor," they answered in clumsy unison.

"All right, then. Let me get to the point. I shall accept the Defense's plea on the charges of drinking underage and disorderly conduct, but I see no basis for the other charges that have been brought against this boy."

"But Your Honor!" Mathews objected.

"Charlie, I'm talking." In a moment of tense silence, Bickford drew his hand down over his chin. Then he said, "Let me tell you what I think happened here. The arresting officers were so upset with this boy for getting the jump on them, for injuring them, that they threw the book at him, and you couldn't tell them they had no case."

"Your Honor, I protest. That's unfair." Mathews was beet red.

"Of course it's unfair, Charlie. You got stuck with a dog that won't hunt while you were still new enough in the office for people to think they could push you around."

Mathews didn't know whether to be comforted by the judge's understanding of what had happened or indignant at this kind of disclosure in front of the defense counsel.

Bickford continued, "Why, I can probably recite half of the conversations about this case that took place over cattle chutes and pickup trucks long before anybody ever even got to your office. Hell, I share some of their sentiments.

We can't let this mountain thing continue to disrupt our community... we can't let anybody challenge the authority of the law...

"And, young Deputy Jenkins looks like some Yankee ice hockey player, for God's sake."

Perkins made the mistake of chuckling at the last comment.

"You sit quiet, Mr. Perkins. I'll get to you." Turning back to Mathews, the judge concluded, "So, the bottom line is this, Charlie: Unless you have neglected to present some profoundly damning piece of evidence, I'm telling you that you don't have a case. No point would be served by pursuing these charges and, if you do, the publicity restrictions to protect the minors would not be sufficient to protect your office or the Sheriff's from embarrassment. How the community sorts out its feelings on this case is not my concern. I'm not going to waste the time of the justice system by proceeding with a trial."

Perkins' satisfaction with this announcement, however unconventional, was short-lived as Bickford bought space for Mathews to cope with his setback by turning on the defense council.

"Now. Mr. Caldwell Perkins, LLD. Your have-gun-will-travel style is not welcome in my court. And lest you take snide comfort from my chiding of Mr. Mathews, let me remind you that you operate in a very privileged position in our system. You are not subject to public election. You don't spend your life arbitrating between the bench and the police, knowing that you can't make them both happy. And your kids don't go to the same school as offspring from both sides of the courtroom. You have correctly divined the weakness in this case, but it was sufficiently obvious that you should take no satisfaction from that accomplishment."

Perkins sorely wanted to respond but, as Bickford began to speak again and the moment passed, he was immediately grateful for the control to have resisted. There was a certain balance to what had just happened and anything from him would have no doubt sent the judge off on another tirade.

"So, gentlemen, let me tell you what's going to happen. In a few moments, I am going to the restroom to relieve myself in a manner not without symbolic value at this juncture. In my absence, you are going to negotiate a plea bargain. I am not at liberty to tell you what that settlement will be, but you now know my views on the matter and you are going to reach an agreement that meets with my acceptance in the appropriate forum. Do I make myself clear?"

Again, the clumsy unison, "Yes, Your Honor."

"Good. I believe a period of ten minutes should do nicely for both our purposes."

Judge Wallace T. Bickford III rose and moved toward the door. Then he stopped and, without looking back, asked, "Incidentally, what is young Fletcher's selective service status?"

* * * * *

The hearing resumed an hour later. Despite the pending formality of the judge's ruling, the mood in the courtroom was more relaxed than it had been the previous week. Perkins had told the Fletchers of his plea agreement and Mathews had begun to feel relief at not having to take his case to trial. Jerry would plead guilty to drinking underage and disorderly conduct, but the other charges would be dropped.

There was still concern that the judge might make some gesture toward the prosecution by ruling on the high side in terms of the sentence. Perkins had told the Fletchers that, if the judge was moved by the severity of the beatings Jerry had dished out, the worst they could expect for Jerry was six months in juvenile detention. On the other hand, and this is what he was hoping for, Bickford could sentence him to probation and perhaps community service.

The recording of the plea and the judge's acceptance amounted to a three-minute formality, but as everyone's attention focused on the judge and his sentencing speech, tension mounted again.

"Mr. Fletcher, do you have anything to say for yourself before I pass sentence?"

It sounded so much like the end of a Perry Mason episode that a moment passed before Jerry realized that he was actually supposed to respond. He had rehearsed a short statement with Perkins, but his attorney had to prod him to stand and it took the full time of awkwardly getting to his feet for him to regain control and begin to speak.

"No, sir, Judge. Well, Yes, sir. One...." He rubbed his hand through his hair. "I know I shouldn't have fought, sir, or drunk. I'm sorry for hurting those people. It won't happen again." Jerry hesitated a moment and then sat down.

"Stand up, Mr. Fletcher, and pay close attention to what I am going to tell you." Bickford had moved without announcement into his sentencing statement.

"There is absolutely no excuse for what you did. I don't care what taunts might have been thrown at you, and I don't care what you may think happened to your family in 1935. This is 1966. There's no place for lopsided versions of history in this community or for the kind of anger they might create. The good people of this community were right to want to see you punished. It is your good fortune that errors were made in assembling the case against you, but if you pull a stunt like this again, I'll be waiting for you."

Perkins was livid with this blatant display of bench prejudice, but he forced himself to remain silent. Any outburst on his part would have triggered a reaction by Bickford that would not be in his client's interest.

"Your school record," Bickford continued, "and your lack of prior encounters with the law lead me to think that the interests of the community are best served by keeping you in school until it is time for you to serve your country. I am therefore sentencing you to six months in juvenile detention, this sentence to be suspended on condition that you remain in school, that you maintain passing grades through the remainder of the academic year, and that you then report for your military service on the first induction date thereafter. Your failure to comply with any of these conditions will result in your immediate arrest and incarceration for the full term of the sentence."

After a moment's silence, he concluded. "Are there any questions?"

CHAPTER 15

David reached through the window of the old Chevy to greet the ranger on duty at the entrance to the Park. Drops of cold rain struck the sleeve of his flannel jacket and glistened in the nap as he shook Charles Jarvis's hand.

"This isn't the weather I had in mind for a walk," he said. "Can't you do better than this?"

"Too wet for ducks, too cold for dogs," Jarvis replied. "Are you sure you want to bother going out there today?"

"Oh yeah. I may not stay too long, but you know how it is. Once in a while a few hours up here can do a fella a lot of good."

"Since I know you're talking about the mountains and not the job, I have to agree."

They both grunted, each recalling his own litany of foibles in the Park Service. Charles was going to retire next year, so he had over thirty years of agency quirks to draw on. He was an institution in the Park Service but it's a good thing he hadn't had any career ambitions. His bluntness with bosses and his carelessness with paperwork would certainly have preempted any promotion that was more than recognition for his intimate knowledge of the Park.

"Well, if you're going to get wet you might as well at least start out warm," he said. "C'mon in here and set by the stove a while." He gestured toward the back of the kiosk where a wood stove sat between two chairs.

David would just as soon have kept going, but he knew he couldn't decline the invitation. It would just be for a few minutes, he assured himself, so he turned the Chevy into the staff parking area and, lifting his jacket over his head, made his way back to the kiosk.

As he opened the back door the warmth enveloped him, and he realized how chilled he had become on the way up from town. Winter brought out the worst in machinery and the old Chevy was no exception. It was holding up well enough in terms of starting on cold mornings and getting him where he needed to go, but the heater was barely functional. It certainly couldn't compete with the draft from the vent windows that he needed to keep open on wet days like this to keep fog from forming on the inside of the windshield.

"I like what you've done with the place," he said as he looked around, rubbing his hands together.

The counter at the front window with materials ready for visitors hadn't changed, but the stove had become the focal point of the room. A set of hooks on the wall next to the stovepipe served as a drying rack for outer clothes. There was a kettle on the back corner of the stove and, on the wall next to it, a shelf held the makings for coffee and hot chocolate.

"Kind of homey, don't you think?" Charles replied, winking, as he reached toward one of the chairs and removed a piece of waxed paper with a half-eaten sandwich.

There were very few visitors to the Park this time of year. The campsites were closed, as were the lodges and restaurants. On weekends there were a few hardy day-hikers and there were always through-travelers wanting to include a section of Skyline Drive in their itinerary. But the load was light, and the small permanent Park Service detail was operating in a relaxed mode. David had noticed sawdust on the sleeve of Charles' uniform coat, hanging by the stovepipe, and there was at least a couple days' stubble on that chin. Superintendent Swan would not have tolerated that, even in mid-winter, but he was somewhere in the Keys on his annual fishing trip.

"So how are things on the morning side of the mountain, my boy?" Charles asked as he took the empty chair and proceeded to re-light the pipe that was his constant companion.

"Pretty good I guess." David settled onto the other chair. "Kind of hectic these days, what with trying to finish school assignments, plan for next year and keep up the church commitments."

"Just the kind of stuff to make a fellow want to go for a quiet walk once in a while," Charles commented. His tobacco was probably some local mix. It could be too pungent in close quarters for some people, but it had an earthy quality that gave the kiosk the smell of an old cabin with a peat fire banked in the hearth.

The conversation meandered through topics of local interest as the two men collaborated on making fresh coffee.

"Which way you heading?" Charles asked, returning to his seat.

"Oh, I don't know. I thought maybe I'd drop down opposite Meadow Spring Trail and walk along the east side a bit."

"You mean toward the old Fletcher place?"

"Yeah, I'll cut through Fletcher Hollow at some point." David answered.

He was distracted momentarily by the personal context Charles had given to the stone chimney that now stood alone and overgrown in a hollow on the eastern slope of the Pinnacle. Hollows often carried peoples' names and for all he knew that could be a vague reference to somebody who passed through there once. But *the old Fletcher place?* That meant someone's home.

After a few moments he asked, "So, you mean people by the name of Fletcher used to live where that old chimney is now?"

"It weren't carved by no glacier. Fletchers built the chimney and the house around it. Fletchers lived in that house for over a hundred years."

David began to picture the place as it might have been.

"It doesn't look like much now," he said, "but it must have been hard to give it up."

"It was hard," Jarvis replied. "It took the Sheriff's Department and the Civilian Conservation Corps to force old Jake and his family to leave."

Now a faded bit of history had a first name as well as a family name and David put things together.

"Is that the same Fletchers that now live over in Flint Hill?" he asked.

"The same, my boy. Gerald Fletcher who runs Fletcher's Motors, he was just a kid when they took him off the mountain."

It suited Charles not to volunteer the additional information that, as a new recruit, he had been part of the Park Service crew that went back that winter morning and burned the Fletcher place down. After all, he had been acting on orders. They had said it was to restore the original condition of the Park. But still, thirty years had only slightly dulled the twist in his gut every time he remembered watching that house go up in flames. He shifted, cleared his throat, and tapped his pipe against the leg of the stove.

"How about a refill?" he asked, standing and busying himself at the stove even before David could answer.

"No. No thanks. I'm fine." David's mind was still on his classmate Jerry Fletcher and what it must be like to have that kind of heritage coursing through him. "The coffee was great," he added.

"But if I'm going to go, I'd better get started." He pulled his jacket back on and gathered his hat and gloves as Charles gave him an update on trail conditions east of the Pinnacle and told him not to be a stranger.

The rain had stopped for the moment but when the door closed on Charles and the stove, David shivered in the damp air.

As he made his way south on Skyline Drive the rain couldn't seem to make up its mind, drizzling one minute and stopping the next, as clouds embedded in the overcast moved across the Ridge.

A mist shrouded the Drive and the surrounding terrain so there was no view of the Shenandoah Valley to the west, where the weather was coming from, or eastward into the Piedmont country that would eventually escort the clouds to the Chesapeake and the sea. The visible world was a hundred yards of rock ledges and wind-stunted oaks on either side of the wet, winding band of pavement.

The old tires had very little tread left and there was always the risk of ice up here this time of year, so David took it easy on the tight turns. With the hat and winter coat he had on the back seat, he wasn't concerned about a little rain. The day would be more enjoyable if he could see a bit of scenery as he walked, but not once did it occur to him to change his plans. He was at ease in the Park and he needed the time alone.

There were no other cars in the parking area at the head of the Meadow Spring Trail. He wasn't surprised to be the only visitor on a day like this, and it suited him. The rain was intermittent and light now, so he got out and put on the winter coat. With the flannel jacket he already wore, he was well insulated against the damp and cold. The peaked cap, with its pull-down ear flaps, completed the protection. He locked the car and slung a light backpack over his shoulder. Pulling a pair of work gloves from an outer pocket, he crossed the road and started east, the mist receding before him as he headed along the gently sloping path toward the shoulder of the mountain.

It was the end of March and, even though the weather hadn't warmed noticeably at this elevation, the winter buds had begun to swell on the oaks, giving them the quality of knots in fine lace against the gray overcast. Beneath the oaks, groves of mountain laurel huddled together against the cold. At their feet, patches of moss and lichen stood out from the drab carpet of dead leaves, their silvers and greens vibrant in the muted light.

After about thirty minutes David emerged from the mature trees that had surrounded the path up to that point and moved into newer growth along a shallow slope. As he walked, the old Fletcher chimney came into view through the mist. With its stones and mortar soaked by the rain, it was darker than he remembered, more substantial. The scattered trees that had grown nearby were taller than the chimney, but they deferred to it in what amounted to a small clearing around its base. Summer weeds that thrived in the reflected heat of this space had been compressed by the snow and softened by the rain until they were now just a tangled mat at David's feet as he sat on the hearth.

Looking out over what had been the Fletcher's front yard, he recalled what Charles had said. "It took the Sheriff's Department and the CCC to force old Jake and his family to leave."

In the shadowy forms and close quarters of the mist, it didn't take much imagination to see the struggle or to feel the loss, the loss of being driven out.

James still hadn't talked to him beyond routine civilities. In fact, since their confrontation at the job site, they seemed even more distant from each other. David had known his father would be upset with his decision to go to university, but it seemed to have virtually cut the ties between them. Shouldn't there be more than theology and career choice between a father and his son?

He wished he could talk to his father as just a man. Surely God wouldn't mind if they talked for a while—like two ordinary men—no scripture, no doctrine. Hadn't his father been young once? Didn't he have the same kinds of questions and doubts that David was going through? And if he did, how did he resolve them? Did prayer answer them, or did it just make them less important? Surely there was some way to lead a righteous life and still explore the mind and the universe God gave us.

He remembered once again standing alone in that room as his father walked away, and tears formed in his eyes as they had a dozen times since that night. He pressed both hands tightly against his face, drawing them down slowly over his eyes and mouth. Then, with a shake of his head, he stood up and strode briskly away from the chimney.

Crossing the old garden patch, he picked up a path, still in evidence, that led uphill toward the southwest. The methodical rhythm of his arms and legs as he walked began to restore him to the present.

The rain had stopped again, and a slight breeze suggested that the low cloud cover might begin to break up. Reaching the protection of larger trees at the edge of the former clearing, he stopped to re-button his outer coat. From beneath a large cedar tree, he looked back in the direction of the old homestead but the chimney where he sat moments earlier had all but disappeared in the mist.

After several minutes, David came to a point where the path circled around a small pool. He knew it was probably spring fed, but at this time of year it was also part of a channel for surface run-off and the current rains had filled the little pool to overflowing.

A stream of clear water, a few inches wide, had cut its way through the path to tumble on down the hillside. Protruding from the far side of this new cut was what appeared to be a small wooden tool. He pulled it from its mud and leaf grave and saw that it was half of a gourd hollowed out to serve as a ladle. One side had broken away and the rawhide strip in its handle fell apart as he tugged at it but, taking it by the handle and turning it in a scooping motion, he could see the role that it and this pool had played in the Fletcher family. He rinsed the ladle off in the pool and put it in his backpack.

Over the next hour, he covered about two miles. Sometimes the trail rose and fell as it crossed the ridges and valleys that made up the mountain's eastern flank. At other times it followed the contour, turning into the face of the mountain along one side of a ravine and then swinging back toward the east.

Even in such rough terrain, the rhythm of walking had a calming effect and David settled into the mental drift that drew him time and again back to these paths. But as he reached a level stretch of the trail, he came upon a message that demanded his full attention. There, in the middle of the path, was a large deposit of fresh bear scat. Coming out of their caves at this time of year, bears are hungry and cranky, and by the size of these droppings, he knew they had been left by a large male.

The wet leaves and soft ground meant that he had been moving more quietly than usual and now he realized that he would have to start making some noise to avoid a surprise encounter with the bear. He looked around until he found a smooth stone about three inches across. He put it in the pocket of his coat, then retrieved the ladle from his backpack and tapped it against the outside of the pocket. The single layer of nylon between it and the rock did little to dull the noise, while the shape of the instrument amplified the sound. Slapping the ladle against his pocket sent a low-frequency beat echoing across the terrain ahead of him.

He dabbled with a marching cadence for the first few minutes while the instrument still amused him, but it soon settled into the background of his mind while random strokes against the pocket continued to serve their purpose. The overcast had indeed begun to break up. Through the trees he could catch glimpses of Old Rag Mountain and, beyond it, the rolling fields and woodlots of Madison County. His spirits brightened with these new vistas, and with the peace of mind afforded by his noisemaker.

The step down over a small rock outcropping was no more difficult than a dozen he had already negotiated. He would have time later to wonder what went wrong but in that moment all he knew was that, as his left foot reached the uneven ground below the drop, it began to roll, and he heard the sickening snap. He pitched forward in freeze-frame consciousness and the first pain struck him like a flash of light before he reached the ground.

One hand and shoulder caught the edge of the trail, flipping him over the side of a steep slope. By the time he came to rest against a tree below the path he had suffered numerous cuts and bruises, but the impact had numbed those even as they happened. He was aware only of the intense waves of pain that pulsed from his left ankle to envelop him as he lay on his back, twisted around the trunk of the tree.

He lay still for several minutes and the throbbing began to ease but, when he tried to breathe deeper than the shallow puffs that had sustained him since the fall, he became aware of pain in his ribs. He would have to get his weight off the tree trunk and into a position where he could lie flat. Groping uphill with his left hand he found an exposed root and tested it with a firm pull. It held. As he rolled slowly toward the uphill arm trying to grip the root with both hands his foot toggled like a broken switch and he let out a scream as it flopped against the hillside. After another pause to let the pain subside, he reached for a nearby branch and pulled himself into a sitting position.

The effort exhausted him and, as his head drooped forward, a tightness developed in the back of his throat and began to extend to his stomach. The thought of what retching would do to his ribs and leg made him fight the nausea. He lay back against the hillside again, hoping that rest and some steady breathing would make the feeling pass. The tension in his stomach eased, and he drifted into sleep for a few moments only to awaken to a sharp jab of pain as he slipped downhill.

Cold and wet, looking about as if to find something to cover himself, David gradually put the pieces of his situation together.

He was ten feet below the trail, four or five miles from the car, cold, wet, and not in good shape to travel. In the drowsiness, he recognized the first signs of shock. If he didn't get this leg working again right quickly, he could be in trouble.

By holding the injured leg in the air with his thigh muscles he could avoid the sharpest of the pain as he pulled himself into a standing position against the tree trunk. His ribs complained but they did their job.

"There, that wasn't too bad," he said aloud, looking up the slope to scout the next stage of his plan. "Now if I just put this foot down squarely—"

He screamed as the ankle gave way and he pitched forward into the wet leaves.

The next fifteen minutes passed in bouts of pain, faintness, and determination as he worked his way up the bank. Once he reached the trail, he looked around for a stout stick to lean on. The winter storms had provided a good candidate within reach, so he was feeling confident as he pulled himself into a standing position again and prepared to test the new stick.

The stick did just fine, but the ankle collapsed with the first ounces of pressure and again he fell on his face, his pain peppered with frustration. But, for the first time there was something else: a twinge of fear, as he realized that he was in trouble.

He pulled himself to a small ledge on the upside of the trail and began to think things through. In the very least, he was going to have to rest for awhile and let the ankle settle down before attempting to walk again. Then he would try to find a bigger stick, one with a 'Y' so he could use it for a crutch. Fortunately, the backpack had not fallen off when he fell, so he still had the water flask and a Hershey bar.

His ribs were letting him breathe almost normally now and there was no longer fresh blood trickling down his face, so he decided that his other injuries weren't serious. The problem was going to be this ankle. He recognized that the snapping noise as he fell had been ligament, not bone, strung taught and released, like the strap on an old slingshot. He shook his head to erase the image of Butch Tolbert, the right tackle who spent the rest of the season on crutches after the same thing had happened to him during a practice last fall.

If he could get to the point that the ankle would accept some weight, he would be able to move toward the Drive. His best bet would be to find Hannah Run and climb out beside the stream bed. It would be steep, and he'd be on his hands and knees a good part of the way, but it was the shortest route to the Drive where he could hail a passing car.

The other problem was the weather. It looked like the clearing would continue but everything on the ground was wet and it was too late in the day for any rise in temperature. As David sat there without moving the breeze chilled his damp clothes and he began to shiver. He managed, with some effort, to pull the groundsheet from his backpack and arrange it so he sat on one edge and had the rest wrapped around his back and shoulders.

He wasn't hungry but what started out as a sip from his canteen threatened to become a torrent until he forced himself to stop mid-gulp to conserve the remaining water. *Maybe a nap will help the ankle,* he thought, and he had no trouble convincing the rest of his body that it was worth a try. He lay back and closed his eyes.

David had no idea how long he'd been asleep, but he awoke with a sudden start. Something heavy was moving along the path, still out of sight around a large outcrop, shuffling and snapping twigs were definitely coming his way. *The bear,* he realized, as the noise that had invaded his sleep took control of his senses.

It's all well and good that black bears are generally timid, he cautioned himself, *but they are also opportunists.*

This one would be hungry at this time of year, and if he sensed weakness there was no telling what he might do. David would have to make threatening noises and gestures to let the animal know that he wasn't looking at an easy victim. This had worked for him several times but on those occasions he had two good legs and a Park Service pickup truck to retreat to in case the gestures failed.

He heard the shuffling again. Closer. If this bear was as large as he guessed, it could be looking down at him as it came around the outcropping. Too vulnerable. Should he shout now, or would that just draw the bear's attention to his vulnerable state? In an instant, he knew what he had to do. He would stand to get a positional advantage over the bear. Then, as it came around the rock, he would raise the groundsheet to create as large a profile as possible and shout at the top of his lungs. The shock should put the bear to flight.

There was no time for what-ifs or then-whats. He struggled to his feet, but a sharp pain pierced his ankle and he twisted away from the path. Behind him, he heard a branch snap and knew the sound had not traveled around the rock.

The bear was there. He had to act now.

With energy born of terror, he raised his cape, spun around, and shouted in the same instant, creating as fearful a phantom as ever stalked a woodland trail.

CHAPTER 16

Jerry Fletcher was tired and inattentive after two days of hunting in the damp and cold. As he rounded the rock outcrop, David's sudden appearance slammed his senses and the weight of his backpack toppled him over the lip of the trail.

The apparition also collapsed to the ground, his chest heaving, his ankle screaming.

For several moments, neither hiker could overcome the adrenaline to begin an exchange. Jerry began to make his way back up the bank, ferrying the backpack in front of him.

As his head appeared above the edge of the path David said, "Boy, am I glad to see you."

"Yeah? You've got a hell of a way of showing it. What the fuck are you doing out here?" Jerry was angry at being frightened, but he was also upset with himself for having been taken by surprise. He was tired but that was no excuse. What if this had been a ranger?

"I was just going for a walk," David answered, and then added, "I thought you were a bear."

"I didn't know what the hell you were. You scared the shit out of me."

"Sorry about that but I was desperate. There was a big pile of fresh bear grease back up the trail and, as you can see, I'm in no shape to entertain that kind of company."

"I saw the bear about an hour ago. He was a big mother," Jerry replied. Then, looking at the leg lying flat on the ground he added, "Got yourself in a bit of a fix, didn't you? What happened?"

"Oh, my mind was someplace else, I guess. I put a foot wrong coming off that ledge." David nodded in the direction of the rock outcropping on the path.

"Can you stand on it?"

"No. I thought I could, but it just won't take any weight."

"Well, it's a long way home on your ass. Better take the downhill route." He moved forward. "Let me take a look," he said, kneeling beside the leg. He wasn't going to be able to tell much by looking, but it would give him some time to think and to adjust to the fact that his own plans would have to change now, too. He resented the imposition but this guy needed help.

The simplest solution would be to make David comfortable and go for help but Jerry couldn't afford to have anyone asking questions about his cargo, and who knows what a curious game warden might do if he began to wonder about somebody wandering around out here this time of year. Until the rain and scavengers had had a chance to finish cleaning up his field dressing sites he didn't want anyone in this part of the Park.

The fresh meat in his backpack would probably be OK for an extra day at these temperatures, but he'd have to secure the pack against the scavengers. The immediate problem was to keep David from asking too many questions. He'd leave the pack where it was for now and focus on getting David sorted out. Once he got him moved a ways up the trail, he'd find some excuse to come back and suspend it between a couple of trees. Then, when David was back on top of the Ridge— probably tomorrow, the way things looked—he'd return for the backpack and leave the Park a different way.

That was enough of a plan for now. He didn't bother about the camping side of things, the getting warm and getting some sleep and food. That was all second nature to him, and he'd see what progress they could make in the remaining hour of daylight before sorting it out.

David's leg had swollen so much that the woolen sock was stretched above the boot top. With that kind of damage, there was no way he would be putting any weight on the foot today.

"Might just as well take your boot off," Jerry said. "That foot's no good to you today, support or no support, and, when we move, the weight of the boot will just twist your ankle."

"Would you mind taking it off for me?" David asked. "I want to barf just thinking about it."

Even with the laces completely out and pulling on the open boot from directly below the foot, Jerry couldn't avoid causing pain that had David on the verge of passing out. Finally, the foot came free. Then the relief as it swelled and blood from ruptured veins seeped into the flesh below the skin. David reached down to touch the spongy surface and rubbed it gently to relieve the itch as the swelling continued.

"You're going to have a souvenir of this one for a while," Jerry said as the two of them watched the foot with fascination.

"Well, that's all OK, but there's the little question of getting out of here," David responded. "And the last thing in the world you wanted was to be stuck with a gimp ten miles from nowhere."

"Oh, relax. It's only six miles, and I didn't have a hot date tonight anyway." Jerry certainly didn't feel that cheerful about it, but what else could he do?

In the few places where the trail was wide enough, David put his left arm over Jerry's shoulder and used him as a crutch, holding the injured foot off the ground. That worked well because David was three inches taller than his rescuer. Where the trail was narrow but fairly level, he could reach over Jerry's shoulders from behind, grasp his wrist with his opposite hand, and Jerry would move forward hauling him along behind him like a travois. David outweighed Jerry by at least thirty pounds so, with either of these techniques, despite Jerry's strength, they could only go fifty yards or so between breathers. Where the trail was steep, David would scoot himself along on his butt, using his arms and one good leg, backward uphill, forward down.

After forty-five minutes of these maneuvers, they were both exhausted, it was almost dark, and they had covered less than a mile. Jerry had hoped to avoid revealing his knowledge of the area, but the situation was serious enough that he made a decision.

"It looks like we're here for the night," he said.

"I guess you're right," David acknowledged, "but all I've got is this one piddling little groundsheet, and everything's too wet to build a fire."

"Don't you fret, son. Uncle Jerry's got a plan. Come on. Haul your ass. We've got another 100 yards to go and most of it's straight uphill."

David was too tired to argue even if he had had any other ideas, so he put his arm over Jerry's shoulder for a short distance along the trail and then began to crawl and skid as Jerry led the way straight up the steep hillside. At standing height, there would have been no evidence of a way through the dense maze of brush and saplings, but from his perspective, David could see that they were following an overgrown path. He also noticed that Jerry was careful to bend branches out of their way and not break them. *Fletcher,* he thought to himself. *Of course. This is his country.*

Their progress was halted when they reached the base of a much steeper slope, its rock outcroppings and overgrown ledges anchored in a mixed tangle of shrubs and small trees. Jerry stepped sideways into the bushes and, leaning back, exposed the entrance to a cave. It was about three feet wide at its base and rose to his waist.

"After you," he said, smiling at David like a magician who had just pulled a rabbit out of his hat.

There wasn't much risk of unwanted company in a cave at this time of year. Wasps were dead, spiders and snakes were dormant, but they used a couple of matches from David's backpack to check anyway.

"You don't suppose our friend's old lady is back in there with a pair of cubs, do you?" David asked apprehensively.

"No chance," Jerry assured him, and seeing the ashes of an old fire pit just inside the entrance, David understood Jerry's confidence. No bear would feel safe going to sleep that close to human contact.

"I see this isn't the first time you've been here."

Jerry deflected the comment, saying simply, "It's good to have a place to go when the weather turns bad."

Working in the dark, from memory, he retrieved some wood from a stockpile a few feet back in the cave, and in a couple of minutes, a small fire flickered in the fire pit. Its light reflected off the walls and ceiling of a chamber about six feet wide and four to six feet high. The back wall appeared to form about ten feet from the entrance, but it had a hole at its base the size of a barrel.

"How far back does this cave go?" David asked.

"It stops there," Jerry replied.

David had already noticed that the smoke from the fire didn't leave by the mouth of the cave but drifted back toward the rear and disappeared into the small opening. That was no dead end but if Jerry didn't want to talk about it, this was certainly not the time to press him.

"I have an idea for your foot," Jerry said, changing the subject. "I'm going out for a couple of minutes and while I'm gone I want you to dig a shallow trench in the dirt to rest your leg in."

He returned carrying two stout sticks in front of him that cradled a load of wet leaves and moss.

"Rest your leg in the trench and pull up your pant leg," he instructed.

David recoiled at the cold as Jerry carefully packed the wet mass around the foot and lower leg.

"There's your ice pack," he said, sitting back on his haunches to inspect the job. "If we change it every hour or so we should be able to get the swelling under control."

David was still trying to get used to the cold against his skin, but he had to admire the technique.

"Listen," Jerry said. "I have to go back and get my backpack. You lean back and relax, and keep the fire going about the way it is now. This place will warm up in a little while."

"No problem." David was already feeling the warmth of the fire. "Take it easy in the dark," he said, "and take your time."

"No sweat. And I'll make you a new moss pie when I get back."

David had dozed off by the time Jerry returned but the fire was burning well, so he knew his patient hadn't been asleep long. A half a Hershey bar sat on a flat rock nearby. As Jerry moved the backpack into the cave he brushed against David and the latter awoke with a start.

"Relax. It's just me."

"Where's the rest of your pack?" David asked, noticing that the large top pack that had thrown Jerry off balance on the trail was missing from the wooden rack.

"I only brought what we need," Jerry replied. "I cached the rest of it. I can go back for it any time." He remembered someone saying that the best lies were ninety percent truth. "I see you ate dinner without me."

"Well, I didn't know when you'd be home. Yours is getting cold over there on the table," he said, pointing at the Hershey bar.

"Cute," Jerry grumbled. "You must be feeling better. Let's see how funny you are after some new moss." He pulled two packages of M&M's out of his own bag and flicked one of them at David.

Jerry was a light sleeper and he kept the fire going during the night. Not high, but enough to keep the chill off the air in the cave. David slept fitfully, sound asleep one moment and wide awake the next in the aftermath of a twitch or roll that moved his leg wrong. But with packs for pillows and outer clothing pulled over them as blankets, they were comfortable. Other than crawling outside to relieve themselves, they both rested reasonably well until sometime after dawn. Jerry had decided that they should change the moss pack one more time before trying to make any moves and his return with a new load of cold wet material signaled the end of David's night.

"You travel equipped," he commented as he smelled the coffee bubbling in a small saucepan on the fire.

"First class," Jerry replied. He poured some of the brew into his one cup and handed it to David. "It's got sugar in it already." Then, he set the pan on a cool area of the dirt floor and proceeded to change the pack on David's ankle. When he was done, he retrieved the saucepan and began to sip his share of the coffee directly from its rim.

"This is the second cup of coffee I've had on this trip," David commented. "Yesterday morning Charles Jarvis and I made a cup in the booth at the Park entrance."

"Who's he? One of the rangers?"

Jerry knew very well who Jarvis was. He knew the Park better than any of the other rangers and more than once Jerry had watched from a high vantage point and fretted as Jarvis followed trails that Jerry thought were known only to him. He had the dubious honor of appearing in Jerry's rifle sights more than any other ranger.

"Yeah, he's a ranger, but he's about to retire."

"Good," Jerry replied, before realizing that he had said anything. "I mean he must be looking forward to retirement." He reached into his pack and produced a plastic container filled with trail mix. "Here," he said, tossing it toward David. "The old lady goes a bit heavy on the raisins, but it's not bad.

"So, what were you doing out here in this kind of weather anyhow?" Jerry's tone wasn't critical, just curious.

"Stuff was piling up on me and I needed to try and clear my head. You don't need good weather for that."

"I thought prayer was supposed to be the way you preachers took care of your troubles."

"Well, it usually helps." David fielded the comment in a matter-of-fact tone. If it was a dig, that would deflate it; if it was a serious comment it deserved an answer. "But maybe it didn't help in this case because the problem is that I've decided not to be a preacher."

"Whoa," Jerry exhaled. "That's front-page news."

"I'd just as soon you didn't make a big deal out of it when we get back."

"Ain't none of my business," Jerry responded when what he really thought was *there's no way I'm going to admit to anyone that I give a shit what you do.* To David, he continued, "But it did sort of seem that that's the direction you were headed."

"Yeah, I thought so, too. But when it came down to it, I discovered that I don't have the commitment to the ministry. What I really want to do is go to college."

"I bet that went over big with your old man."

"He acted like he'd been hit between the eyes."

"Seems to me he should have kept an open mind until you'd had a chance to decide for yourself."

David flinched at this criticism of his father despite the fact that he felt the same way.

"OK, so college, and then what?"

"I don't know for sure, but this Peace Corps thing looks interesting. I've applied to go to Tech and then I think I'll try to work in some other country for a couple of years."

"So you don't want to be a preacher, but a do-gooder is OK, is that it?"

"I guess that's about the size of it, but I think living and working in a different culture could be a good experience."

"I don't get all this interest in leaving home," Jerry said from behind his saucepan of coffee. Looking around the cave he concluded, "Home suits me just fine."

After a brief pause, David said, "And I wasn't the only one out there in the rain yesterday. Thank God, by the way, but what's your excuse?"

"Well, funniest thing, the ministry's not for me either!"

They both had a chuckle.

"Actually, I come up here a lot," he continued, looking into the fire. "It's kind of part of me."

David hesitated, not knowing whether to admit that he knew Jerry's story or not, but after a moment he said, "Charles Jarvis told me about your family, man. Frankly, I can't imagine anything like that. Like, I mean, OK, you hear about stuff like that in history, but to actually have it happen, to be kicked off your land? I don't know if I could handle that."

Jerry hadn't shown any reaction, so David didn't know what to expect when his words had faded to a halt.

"You know, the funny thing is that I wasn't even born up here, but this high country feels like home."

Charles Jarvis's words, *the old Fletcher place*, echoed in David's ear.

"Must be hard not having a regular place to hang your hat when you're at home" he offered.

"Hell, son, you're sitting in my living room. And I've even got a summer place! Neighbors are a bit ornery sometimes, but you get that everywhere."

The comradery of the rejoinder was a rare sentiment in David's world.

"Your father's probably happy about how you've kept up the family tie to this country."

"Yeah, I suppose," Jerry replied, a little awkwardly, then changed the subject. "Hey, it's nice chatting but time's getting on. We'd best think about moving."

Even with the intermittent cloud cover that remained from the previous day's storm, the sun delivered enough light to the cave entrance that, as Jerry removed the leaves and moss, they could see that the ankle was now half the size it had been last night. The only remaining swelling was near the injury itself, along the outside edge of the joint. The blues and yellows were concentrated there as well, but they radiated to the toes like the fake color in grocery store carnations.

"Man, that's spectacular," Jerry said. "Make sure to get a picture of that when you get home."

"It's gross, is what it is," David replied. "But look! I can move it." He bent his foot back and forth an inch or so.

"That's good news, I think," Jerry said, "but don't try to turn it. We need to bind it. This is your department, Mr. Football Player. I'll cut some strips, but you'll have to remember how they did the injured ankles for games."

David thought back and pulled up a clear image of how the wrapping had been done.

"You won't be needing this groundsheet, will you?"

"Not unless it'll take us more than a day to get out of here," David replied.

"Hey, it's been nice, kid, but I don't think so."

With a few deft slits of Jerry's hunting knife, half the groundsheet was reduced to a series of canvas strips. He stood facing David and, at the latter's instruction, lifted the foot and placed it against his knee.

"Now you need to slowly push forward," David said, "so my toes come back toward the top of my leg. Easy now."

He clenched his fists against the pain but held his leg where it needed to be. When the foot was square to the leg, he had Jerry wrap the binding around a couple of times and then begin a series of figure eights around the foot and ankle. He made sure the knots connecting the strips did not lie next to the injury and, moving alternately up and down over the joint with each pass, he constructed a firm binding. A splinter from the woodpile slipped like a straight pin through the last couple of layers to secure the finished bandage.

They pulled their things together, doused the fire, and moved out of the cave. As soon as they were outside, Jerry picked up two sticks that were leaning against the bushes and held them out to David.

"Here, try these."

They were strong oak sticks, each with a Y at the right height to fit under David's arms.

"When did you make these?" David asked, adjusting them under his arms.

"This morning, while you were getting your beauty sleep. How do they feel?"

David took a couple of tentative steps.

"Not too shabby," he reported. "Now you shouldn't have to carry me."

"We'll see about that," Jerry said skeptically. "It's still a long hike and I don't expect you'll make it too far on your own."

They began to make their way down to the trail with Jerry in the lead, carrying the crutches.

"I think we'll climb up by the old Corbin Cabin Trail," he said. "It's a bit longer but it's not as steep as Hannah Run."

"Suits me," David answered, as he slid along the wet ground. Jerry frowned at the damage David's butt was doing to the ground cover as they descended, and he decided that he would have to come back later to scatter some leaves and bend branches back across the path. This place suited him only so long as it remained hidden.

The crutches were rough, but they worked well and the first couple hundred yards on the trail passed quickly as David swung the sticks confidently and the bandage protected the ankle. He didn't pace himself, though, and soon the blood pumping through the suspended foot began to swell the joint again and it throbbed against the bandage. His gloves protected his hands, but the crutches were too narrow to carry his weight comfortably and they began to wear his armpits raw.

"Whew," he said, pausing for a break. "This isn't going to be as easy as I thought."

"Just take it slow," Jerry replied. "We have lots of time. We can stop for breaks whenever you want. My guess is we'll make the Drive by early afternoon."

The morning passed in a series of climbs and breaks, with Jerry supporting or hauling David with greater frequency as the crutches continued to dig at David's arms. They were both warm from the effort and David had removed his outer coat and tied it to his backpack. But the woolen jacket shirt was still more than he needed. At one stop, he took it off and held it at arm's length.

"A gift from my parents," he said, absentmindedly.

Then, as Jerry watched, he pulled a knife from his pack.

"I think we need to operate on those crutches," he said, and cut the shirt down the middle. He wrapped the top of each crutch with one of the halves, using the sleeve to tie the final bundle. "There," he said, "I should have done that a long time ago."

A little past mid-day, as they sat on a low rock outcropping, Jerry took two more granola bars from his pack.

"Time for lunch," he said and handed one to David.

"I think I have to take this bandage off," David said, rubbing his foot. "The pressure is killing me."

"You know better than me you can't do that," Jerry said bluntly. "You'll never get it back on and you won't be able to put an ounce of pressure on that foot."

"Yes, sir, Drill Sergeant, sir." David knew Jerry was right. He flicked him a casual salute and managed a smile. After a few moments, he continued, "So I hear you're headed into the service after we graduate."

"Me and the rest of the world," Jerry answered. "Except you college boys." After a moment, he added, "Have to admit, though; I have trouble imagining me and Uncle Sam on the same dance card. That who leads thing could get tricky."

"Good luck with that," David said. "But college is an option for you, too, isn't it?"

"Yeah, that's what Hanby tried to tell me. At least it was an option before I had that little run-in with Judge Bickford."

David didn't pretend not to know what Jerry was talking about. Word always gets around in a small town.

"But I couldn't see spending four years at something I wasn't interested in when I had this two-year option. It wasn't worth it." He was silent for a moment, then said, "Hey, college just gets you a deferment, but aren't preachers exempt from service."

"Yeah, but the way I see it, it wasn't worth it," David instantly regretted the remark. "Of course, it's worth it if you're called into the ministry. It's just that...." He shrugged instead of finishing the sentence.

Jerry chucked a pebble at him. "Never mind, Preacher. Just don't let the bastards grind you down."

When they started moving again the trail began to level out and, at one point, David stopped abruptly at a familiar sound. About a hundred yards away, hidden by trees and rocks, a car was passing. He turned to see Jerry smiling at him.

"Sounds like you missed your bus," he said.

"There'll be others," David answered quietly, suddenly in no hurry to finish the trip. "I don't know what to say, Jerry. I don't know what would have happened back there if you hadn't come along."

"The way I see it, you'd have slept a little colder last night and I'd be up two granola bars."

"And a pack of M&M's," David reminded him.

Jerry scuffed the ground a couple of times with his boot.

"I'm going to ask you a favor," he began. "The Drive's just beyond those trees and someone will give you a lift back to your car. I'm going to break off here and head back for my stuff."

"No problem," David interjected, "But are you up to it today?"

"Just a minute, I'm not finished." He hesitated before continuing. "I don't want you to tell anyone that you met me up here."

"What? That's crazy. I couldn't have gotten out without you. What about these crutches? What about this binding?"

"The crutches are just dead branches snapped off to size. No tools. You could have made them sitting down. The binding is your own groundsheet, wrapped the way you learned in football."

It dawned on David that Jerry had thought this all through. But why?

"Look, Jerry. You saved my butt, man. The least I can do is tell people what you did. That's pretty small thanks."

"There's only one thank you I want and that's for you to forget that I was here."

David scratched his head for a moment and then looked at his friend.

"OK. I can't forget, but I won't tell anyone."

"Good enough. I appreciate that."

They arranged their things and as they stood to head off in different directions David extended his hand toward Jerry. Gripping the tentative response, he asked,

"Jerry, are you OK?"

"Yeah, sure. Up here I'm fine." Jerry shrugged and smiled wistfully.

They had moved off a few feet when he called back to David.

"By the way, that old ladle you were carrying when you fell? It looks like one my old man used to tell me about. If it's all the same with you, I'm going to take it back to him."

The best David could manage was a nod, and the next time he stopped to look back, Jerry was gone.

CHAPTER 17

THE form letter addressed to Gerald Fletcher Jr. had said:

"You are hereby ordered to report
for induction into the Armed Forces of
the United States. Report at 286 Gay
Street, Washington, Virginia, on June
15, 1966, at 7:00 AM for forwarding to
an Armed Forces Induction Station."

The bottom half of the single sheet contained a bunch of small print about dependency claims, life insurance and other items Jerry took no interest in, but one note did catch his attention:

"You may be found not qualified for
induction. Keep this in mind when arranging your affairs."

What a sense of humor, he thought to himself. *I should be so lucky.*

*****

Only five inductees were reporting for duty that morning, but the vacant lot beside the Rappahannock National Bank on Gay Street was a confusion of duffel bags and the scattered clutches of anxious friends and family members. A Gray Line bus was parked at the curb with its baggage doors open and, on the sidewalk next to it, a table had been set up with a couple of chairs that were occupied by men in army uniforms.

The first inductee to be called stood in front of the table, papers in hand. A general hush had settled over the gathering, broken by low-keyed chatter in the family groups and an occasional tearful sniffle, silenced almost instantly by a handkerchief and hardened glances from male family members.

Faith Fletcher had been dreading this day for as long as she could remember. She had always fretted about her son's growing up—about liquor, about cars, about girls. She worried when he was later than usual getting back from the mountains. Somehow, for a mother, those worries came with the territory, but this morning she was giving her son up to something she didn't understand and didn't trust.

The events that, one by one, had brought them to this day were etched in her mind like an unwanted tune. There was President Kennedy appearing on the television in their living room to announce his decision to send advisors to help some country at the other end of the world in its struggle against communism. Then the disturbing film clips began to show up nightly on Cronkite: Street riots, burning villages, soldiers laughing at the camera or lined up in body bags, lethal machinery rumbling past in the background as voice-overs recounted the game's progress and reported the body count like some perverted scorecard.

Kennedy's death had torn people's minds away from the dirty little war and raised hopes in mothers of draft age boys across the country. But President Johnson dashed those hopes within days, announcing his decision to continue Kennedy's Southeast Asia policy.

Then, there was the telephone call with the news that ripped through the county: The first fatality of a local boy, Willie Jenkins.

The funeral procession passing through town, Faith watching furtively through the lace curtains of the front room, catching a glimpse of the gray coffin in the back of the hearse as it rolled slowly down Main Street and turned onto Fodderstack Road, taking Willie to his burial in the cemetery back of the Beulah Baptist Church. And last summer, President Johnson's announcement to retaliate for the attack on US ships in the Gulf of Tonkin. There was something not right about that business in the Gulf of Tonkin but who was she to question the President of the United States? She was a mother, that's who, and you're damned right she was going to question.

But, short of breaking the law, it was inevitable that she would stand here this morning and watch as the Government reached over and took her boy.

No flags on radio antenna, no smart uniforms, were going to make that any easier or any more sensible. She straightened her dress and shifted her bag as she had a dozen times in the previous thirty minutes. She coughed discreetly or reached up to rearrange her hair— anything to distract herself and avoid bursting into tears. The thought of how the men would react to tears gave her brief moments of annoyance and then amusement before returning her to the sadness that in recent days had become her steady state.

A new black Buick pulled up to the curb behind the bus and people shifted their attention to it, some out of curiosity, some glad for the distraction, and they watched as three men in business suits got out.

"Hey, look," said the sister of one of the inductees, "there's Mr. Miller."

"And there's Charles Johnson," added another well-wisher.

The Fletchers were standing off to one side of the lot and Jerry was just as happy not to have been near the newcomers when he recognized the third man as Judge Bickford.

"It's the Selective Service Board," someone realized out loud.

"Wonder where Colonel Jamieson is," observed another, referring to a missing member of the panel.

"Probably at some other collection point. Big crop to take in, now that school's out."

One of the men in uniform approached the three new arrivals, had a few words with them, and then gestured them toward folding chairs that had been hastily opened next to the processing table. Miller and Johnson took their seats while the judge moved in front of the table, looked out over the crowd and smiled.

Then, in a Fourth of July tone, he said, "Good morning, ladies and gentlemen."

He left a pause for people to settle down, even though it wasn't necessary.

"As many of you know, my name is Judge Wallace T. Bickford. I am the Chairman of the Selective Service Board."

The modest applause came only from people standing so close to the judge that it would have been awkward not to clap.

"This is a proud day for our country," he continued, "and it is a proud day for Virginia. All over our state this morning, young men are beginning a new stage of their lives. All over our state, young men are reporting for duty in the service of their country."

Bickford smiled broadly as he turned his attention to the inductees who had been left in limbo with his arrival.

"As I look at you fine young men heading off into a world of challenge and opportunity, I can't help but feel a special pride for our corner of the Commonwealth. Do you know, gentlemen, do you know, mothers and fathers, that our Selective Service District recruited a higher proportion of eligible men than any other district north of Richmond? And what's more, we beat Richmond all to blazes."

He paused, expecting a round of applause, but the only response he received was from the other members of his board. He glanced inquiringly at the silent groups and most looked back, expressionless. Was it the foolishness of these comments under a compulsory draft system that escaped him, or the social inequity of its waiver provisions? Either way, his comments were an imposition on them at a very difficult moment. Some were just confused; others allowed themselves resentment.

"Don't see no Bickfords in the line," one man said, just loud enough to be heard nearby.

The judge broke the awkwardness by continuing, "Well, we know this is an emotional time for you, mothers and fathers, and you may not want to contemplate the bigger picture just at the moment, but suffice it to say that you all are carrying on a fine tradition of the Commonwealth of Virginia, heeding the call to arms in time of need."

A casual observer might have wondered if Bickford wasn't remaining intentionally vague as to the federal or confederate nature of the needs to which he referred.

Turning to the inductees, he concluded, "My colleagues and I will not impose any further on these last few minutes with your families, men. I wish you Farewell and Godspeed."

Bickford walked around the lot shaking hands with a few of the family groups, singling out some of the inductees for slaps on the back, and generally making his presence felt.

His eyes fixed on Jerry for a moment and he nodded in recognition but did not approach the Fletchers. In the meantime, the two soldiers had returned to processing inductees and it gradually occurred to the judge that he wasn't going to get much more mileage out of this crowd. He spoke briefly to the men in uniform, waved good-bye to nearby families, and, with his colleagues, got back into the Buick. By the time their car pulled away from the curb the three had already returned to whatever conversation the stop had interrupted.

As attention shifted from the departing Buick back to family conversations, no one noticed the figure coming up Gay Street, walking with a cane. When he reached the lot next to the bank, David Williams stepped off the sidewalk and moved across the lawn toward the Fletchers, acknowledging others who recognized him as he made his way through the gathering.

"Well, well. If it isn't the gimp," Jerry said, turning toward David with a smile that belied any attempt at indifference. His mother shot him a reprimanding glance for the gimp remark as David extended his hand toward Gerald.

"Good morning, sir. David Williams."

"This is my dad," Jerry said, catching up with the formalities.

"I figured as much," David chuckled, "and Mrs. Fletcher?" he asked, turning to Faith.

"That's right," she said, offering her hand. "You were one of Jerry's classmates, I suppose?"

"Yes, ma'am, I was."

"But I don't recall seeing you around the shop."

"Well, I have to admit, I'm not into cars as much as some of the guys." Looking at Gerald, he continued, "I'm happy as long as mine gets me where I want to go and doesn't complain."

"Don't quote me," Gerald replied. "It would be bad for business. But provided you change the oil once in a while, that's a real smart attitude."

"I try to keep an eye on it," David said, then turned to Jerry. "Are you ready for your bus ride?" he asked.

"Yeah, some kind of bus ride," Jerry replied, rolling his eyes.

"And what are your plans now that school's over," Faith asked.

"It looks like I'll be going to Tech," David said with a grin. "I got my acceptance letter yesterday."

"Congratulations," she said. Gerald echoed the feeling and asked what he planned to study.

"I don't know for sure. Science, probably agriculture."

"That would be interesting," Gerald said and offered the stock endorsement, "People are always going to have to eat."

One of the soldiers called out the name of the next inductee and for a moment everyone watched silently as one of the guys who used to work in the co-op warehouse made his way toward the table.

"What did you do to your leg?" Faith asked. Jerry shot David an anxious glance which he ignored and said, "Oh, I was hiking a couple of months back and I went over on my ankle."

"That'll take the fun out of a hike in a hurry," Gerald said. "I hope you weren't too far away from help."

"No. Fortunately, I was with a friend who was a big help getting me back to the car."

"There, you see," Faith turned to Jerry. "I'm not being silly when I worry about you being off by yourself. Things really do happen."

"OK, Mom. You made your point," Jerry said, then looking at David he added, "Come on. Let's take a walk."

"Don't go far, now," Faith said, "and listen for your name." Jerry threw a conventional yes-mother, if-I-have-to look her way and, for a brief moment she imagined that she was back in the kitchen, just seeing him off for another day at school.

"What brings you around here this morning?"

"Oh, I just wanted to see you off. And I wanted to thank you again for helping me get off the mountain. It turns out I really messed this thing up," he added, nodding toward the ankle.

"They told me it could have been a lot worse if we hadn't gotten the swelling under control. Something about cutting off circulation. Anyhow, it was enough to remind me how glad I am that you showed up."

"OK, but just remember our deal. Nobody needs to know."

David smiled. "Yeah, that was the deal. But there's another part of it I didn't tell you about."

Jerry stopped and turned toward him, "Na-ah, no add-ons. it doesn't work that way."

"In this case it does. You just need to know that if I can ever do anything for you, all you have to do is ask."

"All right. I appreciate that."

"And one more thing," David said.

"You're pushing your luck here, boy." Jerry was feeling awkward.

"Just be careful, will you?"

"No sweat, man." Jerry kept his answer short. "But thanks."

David waived good-bye to the Fletchers and took his leave.

Jerry was relieved when the order finally came to board the bus. He turned to his mother, gave her a hug, and then stood smiling at her while she touched his cheek with fingers damp with her own tears. With a firm shake of his large, calloused hand, Gerald said, "Give 'em hell, son." And that was it.

A couple of miles east of Ben Venue the bus topped a crest and Jerry turned to look back as the Blue Ridge Mountains defined the receding skyline for the last time.

THE STORY CONTINUES IN
FLETCHER'S WAR

ANOTHER TWO ROADS HOME NOVEL
#BairInkBooks #TwoRoadsHome #JamesGBrown

We hope you have enjoyed
The Morning Side
by James G. Brown.

Please post a review with your bookseller,
follow us on social media
and tell a friend.

Find us on social media!
#BairInkBooks #TwoRoadsHome #JamesGBrown

ABOUT THE AUTHOR

Growing up, Jim Brown spent hundreds of hours exploring remote areas of Eastern Canada and the Appalachians. He built a career in agriculture and international finance, traveling to rural areas in developing countries around the world with the World Bank and other international agencies.

In the late 1990s Jim and his wife Camilla settled on a small farm in the shadow of the Blue Ridge Mountains. "When it was time to go to work," he says, "I was only an hour from Dulles Airport but living in a rural setting restored the grounding in nature I had known as a young man."

Currently an adjunct professor of international development policy at the George Washington University, Jim has published articles on life in rural Virginia and books in the field of agroindustry and rural development.

The Morning Side is his debut novel and the beginning of a four-book series entitled *Two Roads Home*.

Made in the USA
Middletown, DE
09 April 2021